THE ROARING QUEEN

WYNDHAM LEWIS

The Roaring Queen

Edited and introduced by Walter Allen

LIVERIGHT · NEW YORK

First published in the U.S.A. in 1973 by
Liveright, 386 Park Avenue South,
New York, N.Y. 10016

Copyright © 1973 by the Estate of the late Wyndham Lewis
Introduction copyright © 1973 by Walter Allen

ISBN: 0–87140–576–8
Library of Congress Catalog Card Number: 73–80783

Printed in Great Britain

INTRODUCTION
by Walter Allen

On 14 April 1936, in a letter to Father Martin D'Arcy, S.J., Wyndham Lewis wrote: 'My short novel *The Roaring Queen* is also now finished and Capes are doing it.' Five months later, the book was listed among the *New Statesman and Nation*'s selected novels for the autumn, but it does not seem to have been advertised either in that periodical or in the *Times Literary Supplement*, though advertising space was found for forthcoming novels by, among others, C. Day Lewis and Stevie Smith. Then, sometime in November, Lewis had a letter from G. Wren Howard, a director of the house of Cape, expressing concern about the possibilities of libel in the novel. Lewis replied, though it is not certain that the letter was ever sent:

> Libels I did not discuss (nor did you, although you are at least as well acquainted with the world I made fun of) because there is no libel there. But in any satire there is always the possibility – indeed almost the probability – that someone or other (either with a grudge against the author, or with a keen business sense and a desire to turn an honest penny) will come forward and claim financial compensation for an alleged 'libel'. What happens then? The publisher, in nine cases out of ten, refuses to go to the court with it, however ill-founded the charge. He just hands over the money to the claimant, if necessary suppresses the book, and that is not only disagreeable for the publisher, but also for the author.
>
> Under these circumstances, and since I myself have been a conspicuous sufferer in that matter, it is only natural that I should wish to have your *absolute assurance* that there was nothing in my book that you would not be prepared to stand by . . .

Your letter, I need hardly say, is disingenuous. For to say in this particular case that you carefully read yourself and accept a book satirizing the world in the midst of which you live – accept it in all good faith, so to speak – and then all of a sudden discover that it is swarming with atrocious libels, is plain nonsense.

At the very start it was open to refuse the book at sight: to say to me: 'Look here, I know the business in which I am engaged has its anomalies and absurdities, like all walks of life, but I am after all engaged in it, and I don't propose to publish satires about it. Besides, I might make myself unpopular with some of my eminent colleagues.' That I should have entirely understood. Indeed, I told you that several publishers had refused it; that in the nature of things the *small* publisher would be afraid of publishing it for fear of offending his big colleagues, and that the big publisher would hardly feel very genial about it . . .

In the event, though Lewis had passed the proofs, *The Roaring Queen* was not published, and the book world, which was the world Lewis was making fun of, has remained undisturbed by it for thirty-seven years. Libel is a matter for lawyers, and whether *The Roaring Queen* was technically libellous I do not know. Most of the characters identifiable in the novel – or presumed by the curious to be identifiable, which is something else – must be dead by now, and some were dead in 1936. But it doesn't need much imagination or much knowledge of human behaviour to realize the controversy and the heat *The Roaring Queen* would have sparked off if it had appeared in 1936. Assuredly, all the characters would have been 'recognized', however weak the evidence, and I find it puzzling to understand Cape's accepting the novel in the first instance. There is, for example, the reference by an anonymous character to 'Geoffrey Bell who is reader for *Hector Gollywog and Ogpu*, who in his capacity of novel-critic of the *Sunday Messenger* writes the most glowing accounts of the books that reach him as critic from the firm to which he belongs, as reader'. Anyone at Cape's must have known that this could only refer to the poet and journalist Gerald Gould, who was for years the chief novel-reviewer of the *Observer*.

Today, of course, after a third of a century, positive identification of the characters in *The Roaring Queen* is much less easy. The only people more quickly and easily forgotten than best-selling novelists are the journalists who review their works, and it is to these categories of human beings that the characters of the novel mainly belong. Indeed, when a positive identification of an original can be made, it can be made, except in one instance, only on the basis of some degree of specialized knowledge that the common reader is unlikely to have. For the other characters, one is largely in the realm of intelligent guess-work, since Lewis, as it seems to me, was often incorporating in a single character traits from more than one original and, still more often, was satirizing not specific persons so much as trends he discerned in literary fashion and in the marketing of books.

The one unmistakable figure, today as in 1936, is the central character, Samuel Shodbutt, who can only be Arnold Bennett, and a very funny caricature of Bennett at that. I think it an unfair one, but that is beside the point: one doesn't expect fairness in satire, and in any case Lewis believed he had justification for his satire. Bennett had in fact been dead five years before the novel was due to be published. Indeed, Lewis dates the action of the novel fairly specifically when he describes Shodbutt as a 'Canute of 1930'. That Shodbutt is meant to be Bennett is clinched by the fact that in the proof copy of the novel there is a page on which the initials A.B. appear instead of S.S.

The aspect of Bennett that Lewis is satirizing is that described by Richard Hughes in an article in *Encounter* in

1963: he is recalling the time when he discovered – and he was the first Englishman to do so – the early novels of William Faulkner:

... Those were the days when Arnold Bennett was running his book-column each week in the *Evening Standard*. Bennett had then a greater influence on book-sales than any other critic before or since (people trusted him particularly because his critical style was so open and commonsensical: it was never his way to puff or over-praise a book, however much it had interested him). Being fresh from America, Bennett asked me one night at dinner what was new there, and scribbled the name 'Faulkner' on his hard evening cuff.

Apparently Bennett wrote off at once to New York ordering the entire Faulkner oeuvre.

Having got them, Bennett wrote a paragraph in his column, as a result of which *Soldier's Pay* and *Mosquitoes* were published in London with Hughes' memorable introductions.

Hughes presents an estimate of Bennett as a reviewer and a maker and breaker of reputations quite different from Lewis'. All they have in common is a recognition of Bennett's enormous power to persuade the reading public to read and perhaps to buy books. Nevertheless, Hughes' article throws some light on an episode in *The Roaring Queen*. When Rhoda Hyman tells how she had plagiarized the novel of an 'unknown American' Shodbutt denies that there can be any such person:

'The Americans are not allowed to neglect their authors – I see to that!' Shodbutt blustered, in a paroxysm of boastfulness. 'That is fairly well known, I think! They can neglect *ours* if they want to. That's another matter. I don't care about that – we do it ourselves!' He chuckled among his long rabbit teeth. 'But I won't have them neglect *theirs* – and what's more they know it!'

It is one of the funniest passages in the novel, and with

Richard Hughes' article beside one, one can see where Lewis could have got it from. Hughes quotes from Bennett's *Evening Standard* review of *Soldier's Pay*:

> Last year I made some fuss in this column concerning the young American novelist, William Faulkner, who had been mentioned to me in conversation by Richard Hughes, author of *A High Wind in Jamaica*. No American, and even no American publisher, whom I asked about Faulkner, had ever heard of him. I sent to New York for his books, but could get only one, *The Sound and the Fury*, and that not without difficulty. Strange that Americans have frequently to be told by Englishmen of their new authors!
>
> The first printed fuss made about Theodore Dreiser's first book was made by an Englishman. *Sister Carrie* fell flat in the United States until a review of it by myself was republished there. Then Americans said: 'Who is this man Dreiser?' and *Sister Carrie* began to sell in America. That was thirty years ago. Yet Americans say that English critics sniff at American novels.

But why did Lewis single out Bennett as the target of his satire? In *Rude Assignment*, an autobiographical work published in 1950, he refers to the 'era of puff and blurb in place of criticism' and says: '*That* started with Mr Arnold Bennett, when he turned reviewer and star-salesman for the publishers, and was the godfather of as fine a brood of third-rate "masterpieces" as you could hope to find anywhere.' He saw Bennett as the arch-representative of the commercialization of literature, of the promotion of book-publishing to big business; though in *The Roaring Queen* he doesn't fail to make the distinction between Bennett the Edwardian novelist and Bennett the all-powerful book-reviewer.

Bennett had in fact been under criticism for several years before his death. Questionings of his achievement as a novelist were almost common form and were a product of what is now called the generation-gap, inevitable at a time when the novelists the young found exciting were Joyce and

Lawrence. Bennett was conscious of this; as he wrote in a letter in 1928: 'I have long been aware that some of the younger generation despise me. (The feeling is not mutual.)' Then, his public presentation of himself could easily be construed as comic and vulgar, self-complacent and Philistine. This side of him was summed up by the poet Roy Campbell, a friend of Lewis', who wrote of him in 1928 that he 'quite openly admits, in the *Evening Standard*, in his weekly tips to young poets, that he places his insurance policy, his clothes and his belly a long way before his brains: and that he considers it a far greater privilege to be Mr Bennett – and pay his grocer's bill, than to be Homer – and die in poverty.' Indeed, as will become clear, a great deal of the comedy of *The Roaring Queen* and of its mechanisms is based upon these attitudes towards Bennett, which were far from being Lewis' alone.

As early as 1920, for instance, he had appeared as Mr Nixon, the book-reviewer, in Ezra Pound's *Hugh Selwyn Mauberley* – Pound was of course a close friend of Lewis'. Mr Nixon has gained a steam yacht from the proceeds of writing, as Bennett had done, and he assures Mauberley, 'As for poetry, there is nothing in it,' and advises him to 'Follow me, and take a column,' as he had done in the years before the first war in the *New Age*, to which both Pound and Lewis had contributed.

But beyond all this, there was a personal basis for Lewis' attack on Bennett, whom he believed had done him down over the years. In a letter to Hugh Walpole written in January 1920, Bennett describes a dinner-party at Osbert Sitwell's:

Very good dinner & the most fantastic and hazardous service. Sickert was there. He is, I regret to say, becoming rather mannered; but his imitations of his old & intimate friend George Moore are still priceless. Wyndham Lewis was also there – in grey flannel. He left early – piqued, as some said, by remarks of Sickert.

Seventeen years later, we have Lewis' version of the dinner party in his autobiography *Blasting and Bombardiering*:

> At this dinner-party Sickert began talking about *Tarr*. I could see Bennett didn't like it. I think Sickert saw that too, for he went on talking about it more and more, at every moment in more ecstatic terms. I did not engage in the conversation. I saw that Bennett was extremely annoyed; and when at last Sickert said: 'Here we've been talking about it for a quarter of an hour. The author has said nothing. But I don't think it matters *what* we say about it, one way or the other!' Bennett threw himself back in his chair at this, and stammered out crossly, 'Oh, I shouldn't say that. I shouldn't say that!'
>
> Naturally it was aggravating of Sickert to make Bennett talk about a 'young author's' book for half an hour. For I saw only too well that as an old hand he had resented this ordeal. So much irresponsible jealousy had been more than he could stomach. *Tarr* had been made to stink in his nostrils. Bennett had an age-complex as big as a house. I knew that Sickert had made me an enemy though he hadn't meant to, for he is the kindest man in the world.

Lewis goes on:

> For a number of years Arnold Bennett was a kind of book-dictator. Every week in the pages of the *Evening Standard* he 'dictated' what the Public should read. And more or less the Public obeyed. He was the Hitler of the book-racket. The book-trade said he could make a book overnight. If he praised it on Thursday evening, by the weekend it was selling like hot cakes. And he became inordinately proud of this accomplishment. He loved power in the way that a 'captain of industry' loves power . . .
>
> The 'author of *Tarr*' under this Dictatorship spent his time in a spiritual concentration camp – of barbed silence. . . . This John Keats would have had much more porridge if this particular Hitler hadn't taken a dislike to the cut of his hair. If Letters were Life,

I am persuaded, I should have been beheaded. My head would have 'rolled in the sand'.

Lewis concludes his account of the episode:

As Sickert and I left the Sitwells that night (in 1922 or 3) I reproached him for having been so vehement with Bennett. But Sickert exclaimed against my retrospective objection. 'Nonsense! Why shouldn't he hear it! Of course he should be told – that and a lot more! *Quel comédie* – that such people as Arnold Bennett should be in a position of that sort – it is only in an age like ours that they could be! That one should have to talk to such people about *books* at all! Why should one be asked to meet such people? It is absurd that a Bennett should be referred to for anything except the time of a train or the cost of a bicycle lamp! Pfui!'

This outburst of Richard Sickert's should be set side by side with the comments on Shodbutt of the painter Richard Dritter. Dritter is plainly based on Sickert, who died in 1942, as is clear not only from the similarity of opinion and expression (certainly not because he is depicted as a painter with a beard, a detail which has led one unwary commentator on the novel to identify him with Augustus John), but also because of the reference to 'his master, Whistler', like whom 'he has a tongue to his credit as well as a brush'.

The Roaring Queen opens with Samuel Shodbutt, chief reviewer of the *Morning Outcry* and chairman of the Book of the Week Club, *en route* to a weekend party at Beverley Chase, the Oxfordshire mansion of the Wellesley-Crooks, there to meet the other potentates of the book-racket, the chairmen of rival book clubs, other reviewers, authors and so on. Before the party is over he will announce the next week's choice of the Book of the Week Club. When he arrives, he meets many old enemies, prominent among them being Mrs Rhoda Hyman. Who is Mrs Hyman? Or rather, who is Mrs Hyman's original? I think there can be no doubt at all that she is, surprisingly, Mrs Virginia Woolf. I say surprisingly because she doesn't fit in, in any way, with what I suspect are our present impressions of Virginia Woolf. She is anything but a speaking likeness and is obviously not intended to be one; and the facts, as we are told, that her father was a literary journalist and that she has associations with Cambridge would certainly not be enough to pin the identity upon her. Yet she is based on Virginia Woolf all the same.

In his presentation of Rhoda Hyman Lewis is doing two things at once: he is dramatizing Bennett's relationship with Virginia Woolf and also expressing his own reactions towards her. Bennett's attitude towards Virginia Woolf, and hers to him, was always ambivalent. In *The Roaring Queen* Shodbutt's first encounter with Rhoda begins:

And if the gaze of Samuel Shodbutt fell more ponderously in one place than another, it oppressed, if anything, more peculiarly that drooping intellect-ravaged exterior of the lanky and sickly lady in Victorian muslins – the greater and more world-famous of the pair of mind-proud, vacantly staring – for no banns ever published would devirginate either of those colossal spinsters. Yes! there, beneath his very eyes, wilted pretentiously the very woman who had but a few months ago written a vile supercilious pamphlet all about Shodbutt. And it had been a very insulting piece of work indeed. So the highly finished languor of the patronizing queen of the highbrow world (whose pen had but yesterday allowed itself to be facetious at the expense of the scribbling grocer puffed up into a Brummagem critical Lion) attracted the darkest sparks from his smouldering eye-socket – and Shodbutt's chin was puckered like a disgruntled patch of ocean ruffled into a snarling surface by a storm – and the drooping extremities of his moustache whiskered dankly the contemptuous corners of his mouth.

Well, Virginia Woolf had indeed written a pamphlet to do with Arnold Bennett, a pamphlet called *Mr Bennett and*

Mrs Brown, published in 1924. It is very amusing. Mrs Woolf reports Bennett as having said 'that there was no great novelist among the Georgian writers because they cannot create characters who are real, true and convincing', and she adds: 'And there I cannot agree.' The Georgian writers are Mrs Woolf herself, Joyce, Lawrence, Forster, Lytton Strachey and T. S. Eliot, and the pamphlet is an attack on her immediate predecessors in the English novel, Bennett, Wells and Galsworthy. It is Bennett, because he has supplied her with her text, who has to bear the brunt of the attack. The Mrs Brown of the title is an old lady sitting in a railway carriage: she is human nature. 'With all his powers of observation, which are marvellous,' says Mrs Woolf, 'with all his sympathy and humanity, which are great, Mr Bennett has never once looked at Mrs Brown in her corner.' Bennett as a novelist is disposed of – in much the same way and to the same degree as the next generation of novelists disposed of Virginia Woolf. But the difference between them was not simply a difference between generations: it was a difference between attitudes towards the art of the novel, and they were both conscious artists dedicated to their literary form. In this sense, they were enemies, for it seemed as though if one were right the other must be wrong. They attacked each other on aesthetic grounds.

At the personal level it was rather different, for there was at least a grudging respect on both sides. On 1 December 1930, they found themselves together at a dinner-party. It had been engineered, Virginia Woolf thought, by Bennett himself to enable him to 'get on good terms' with her. She adds – it is from *A Writer's Diary* – 'Heaven knows I don't care a rap if I'm on terms with B. or not.' She goes on to tell how she drew Lord David Cecil into the conversation. 'And we taunted the old creature into thinking us refined.' It is not a pleasant piece of writing, but that the effect of the meeting on Mrs Woolf was considerable is shown by the fact that, recording it the day after, she says: 'this left me in a state where I can hardly drive my pen across the page.'

We have Bennett's account of the meeting. He wrote to his nephew: 'Last night I was at Ethel Sands' and had a great pow-wow with Virginia Woolf. (Other guests held their breath to listen to us.) Virginia is all right.' One gets the impression that in their encounter the 'old creature', who was sixty-three as contrasted with Virginia Woolf's mere forty-eight, appeared much the more naïve of the two. But a year later, under the heading 'Saturday, March 28', we find this in Virginia Woolf's diary:

Arnold Bennett died last night; which leaves me sadder than I should have supposed. A lovable genuine man; impeded, somehow a little awkward in life; well meaning; ponderous; kindly; coarse; knowing he was coarse; dimly floundering and feeling for some thing else; glutted with success; wounded in his feelings; avid; thicklipped; prosaic intolerably; rather dignified; set upon writing; yet always taken in; deluded by splendour and success; but naïve; an old bore; an egotist; much at the mercy of life for all his competence; a shopkeeper's view of literature; yet with the rudiments, covered over with fat and prosperity and the desire for hideous Empire furniture, of sensibility. Some real understanding power, as well as a gigantic absorbing power. These are the sort of things that I think by fits and starts this morning, as I sit journalizing . . . Queer how one regrets the dispersal of anybody who seemed – as I say – genuine: who had direct contact with life – for he abused me; and yet I rather wished him to go on abusing me; and me abusing him. An element in life – even in mine that was remote – taken away. This is what one minds.

Lewis' attitude towards Virginia Woolf was, I think, much less complex than Bennett's. She was a member of 'Bloomsbury', and his references to Bloomsbury are generally fairly contemptuous, both because it was part of the literary Establishment and because of his intellectual views.

And then she was a friend of the art-critic and painter Roger Fry, who Lewis all his life believed had done him down early in his career as a painter. Before writing *The Roaring Queen*, Lewis had already published a criticism of Virginia Woolf in his book, *Men Without Art*, in 1934. We know from her diary how concerned she was, before its publication, about what Lewis might have written of her. On Thursday, 11 October 1934, she writes:

> A brief note. In today's *Lit. Sup.*, they advertise *Men Without Art*, by Wyndham Lewis: chapters on Eliot, Faulkner, Hemingway, Virginia Woolf. . . . Now I know by reason and instinct that this is an attack; that I am publicly demolished; nothing is left of me in Oxford and Cambridge and places where the young read Wyndham Lewis. My instinct is not to read it . . . Why am I so sensitive? I think vanity: I dislike the thought of being laughed at: at the glow of satisfaction that A., B. and C. will get from hearing V.W. demolished . . .

Three days later, she has either read Lewis' book or the reviews in the Sunday papers:

> This morning I've taken the arrow of W.L. to my heart: he makes tremendous and delightful fun of A.B., Mr Bennett and Brown: calls me a peeper, not a looker; a fundamental prude but one of the four or five living (so it seems) who is an artist. That's what I gather the flagellation amounts to . . . Well, this gnat has settled and stung: and I think (12.30) the pain is over. Yes, I think it's now rippling away. Only I can't write.

Nevertheless, for the next three weeks or so references to Lewis and his book recur in her diary, and perhaps for good reason. On 19 October Stephen Spender reviewed *Men Without Art* in the *Spectator* and wrote that Lewis had attacked Mrs Woolf with a 'great deal of malice', which great deal of malice, Lewis believed, Spender found in his reference to 'the obvious imitation of episodes in *Ulysses* to be met with in *Mrs Dalloway*'. Lewis had written, of these imitations:

> In our local exponents of this method there is none of the realistic vigour of Mr Joyce, though often the incidents in the local 'master-pieces' are exact and puerile copies of the scenes in his Dublin drama (cf. the Viceroy's progress through Dublin in *Ulysses* with the Queen's progress through London in *Mrs Dalloway* – the latter is a sort of undergraduate imitation of the former, winding up with a smoke-writing in the sky, a pathetic 'crib' of the firework display and the rocket that is the culmination of Mr Bloom's beach ecstasy).

This indebtedness of Mrs Woolf to Joyce, which cannot, I think, be denied, is surely the basis of Lewis' making Rhoda Hyman bestow on herself the diploma for the Year's Cleverest Literary Larceny. The comedy is the more farcical when we discover that the larceny is from an unknown American who, it is suggested at one point in the mis-understandings of conversation, may be Sinclair Lewis.

And now we enter into the realms of surmise. I doubt whether at this date other characters can be identified positively. The most one can do is to give reasons for intelligent guesses, in the full knowledge that the guesses may be utterly wrong. According to Mrs Wyndham Lewis, in a letter to the present publisher, 'Nancy Cunard was the main figure in the book.' By this I assume she means Baby Bucktrout. Mrs Lewis goes on to say that 'most certainly she did not object even if she had recognized her satirical portrait'; and it appears that after reading the novel, Miss Cunard wished to publish it at her Hours Press, in France. But Lewis needed an advance on royalties, which was against her practice as a publisher of small editions of *avant-garde* works.

In this, Nancy Cunard's behaviour towards Lewis seems to have been characteristic; but whether one would have spotted Baby as Nancy Cunard without Mrs Lewis' word for it I do not know. There are problems of chronology. In the novel, Baby is a girl in her late teens trying to seduce a young gardener with *Lady Chatterley's Lover*, which was published in 1928, as her primer. In fact, in 1930, the date of the action of the novel, Miss Cunard was 34. Certainly, in a rough-and-ready way, the presentation is in character. Miss Cunard, the daughter of the famous hostess Lady Cunard, was one of the great rebellious figures of the twenties and thirties, a beautiful woman notorious for her flouting of the conventions and her passionate support of left-wing causes, a bohemian when the word still had a meaning. She had known Lewis all her adult life and had sat to him for a portrait. The original of characters of many novels in the inter-war years, among her avatars are Iris March, in Michael Arlen's *The Green Hat*, and Lucy Tantamount, in Huxley's *Point Counter Point*. According to Daphne Fielding, in *Emerald and Nancy*, a memoir of Miss Cunard and her mother, Nancy suffered as a child under the tyranny of a governess named Scarth: one is tempted to equate this lady with Lewis' Miss Corse, who carries Nancy, kicking and biting, under her beefy arm when she is discovered riding piggy-back on the young gardener. And though the seduction episode, with its satire on Lawrence's novel, needs no explanation, it is tempting to relate it to an incident in Nancy's girlhood. According to Daphne Fielding, Miss Scarth discovered that she was reading Elinor Glyn's novel, *Three Weeks*, the wicked book of the period. 'A frightful Rumpus' ensued, from which Nancy was rescued only by the intervention of her mother's great admirer, George Moore.

However, if we can identify Baby Bucktrout with Miss Cunard then we may have some tenuous clue to the identity of the Roaring Queen himself, Donald Butterboy, the homosexual undergraduate whose novel, *It Takes Two to Make a Bedroom-Scene!*, is to be Shodbutt's next choice of the Book of the Week Club. Butterboy is presented so much as the undifferentiated stereotype of the effeminate young man, the 'flaunting, extravagant queen' as one might say, that he could have been based on any number of young men and young novelists of the time. But the modern reader will probably think first of the late Brian Howard, mainly because it is from him that the stereotype of the homosexual as we know it now derives. Michael Holroyd in his life of Lytton Strachey sums him up in the sentence: 'Wit, poet, critic and friend of the famous, Brian Howard dazzled Eton, Oxford and London during the 'twenties and 'thirties by his exotic manner of living and of conversation.' He appears in the novels of Evelyn Waugh as Ambrose Silk in *Put Out More Flags* and as Anthony Blanche in *Brideshead Revisited*, and Waugh describes him in his autobiography as 'mad, bad and dangerous to know'. He did in fact write a poem called 'Two It Takes to Make a Flower', but, alas, it was not written until seven years after Lewis wrote *The Roaring Queen*. Had the novel not been suppressed, it is more than likely that Howard would have reviewed it, since at the time he was one of the fiction-reviewers on the *New Statesman and Nation*. I did not know him, but since he praised my own first novel generously I am bound to think he was a good reviewer. He had also, as a boy of fifteen at Eton, published a satirical piece that takes swipes at Lewis in the *New Age*. There was obviously much more to Howard than appears in Donald Butterboy.

The possible clue to Butterboy's identity is that in the novel Baby Bucktrout is reluctantly engaged to him. I am pretty sure that Nancy Cunard was never engaged to Brian Howard, but that they were close friends is certain. Indeed, at one time, according to Daphne Fielding, she declared that she loved him 'in every possible way'. Miss Fielding goes on:

Though he admired her beauty and respected her idealism, the knowledge of her being physically in love with him was distinctly uncomfortable. As he told his mother, 'Nothing could deter her or make her dishonest. . . . If she were younger and less ill and attracted me, I'd marry her, I almost believe.'

She published his poems from the Hours Press.

Baby is the niece of Mrs Wellesley-Crook, the great hostess of Beverley Chase; and since Beverley Chase is located in Oxfordshire I suppose the mind inevitably turns first to thoughts of Garsington and Lady Ottoline Morrell. I am certain Lady Ottoline was not the model for Mrs Wellesley-Crook, and it seems to me likely that many hostesses went to her making. Part of her, though, is probably derived from Nancy's mother Lady Cunard. Like Lady Cunard, Mrs Wellesley-Crook is American in origin. Lady Cunard came from San Francisco; Mrs Wellesley-Crook has been a 'Crook of Chicago, with a verandahed château in the South, in the Old Dominion, where she was connected with the aristocratic Blackwood Toyts.' Lewis had known Lady Cunard for the greater part of his life and in *Blasting and Bombardiering* he writes of her with considerable warmth. Their first association seems to have been in 1914, when Lewis was running the Rebel Art Centre with the painters C. R. W. Nevinson, Cuthbert Hamilton and Edward Wadsworth. Lady Cunard commissioned them to decorate some handkerchiefs, scarves, candles and fans to be used as favours at a party. It appears to have been the only commission the Rebel Art Centre was offered. Later, during the First War, when Lewis was a subaltern on leave from Flanders, he attended Lady Cunard's dinner-parties and on one occasion, according to Peter Quennell, he was invited to luncheon to meet the Prince of Wales. It must have been a memorable occasion:

Wyndham Lewis accepted the invitation, contrary to his usual practice; but he was taciturn and pensive and self-absorbed, and, as soon as they had sat down to luncheon, produced from his pocket a small pearl-handled revolver, which he placed beside his wine-glasses. Did he mean to assassinate the Prince? Was it his intention to commit suicide? At all events, a crisis threatened; disengaging herself from the guest of honour, she turned her attention at the first opportunity to Mr Wyndham Lewis's 'pretty little pistol', admiring its workmanship and the elegance of the design, handling it as if it had been a Fabergé Easter Egg or an enamelled Georgian snuff-box, at length with an absent-minded smile dropping the weapon into the bag she carried; after which she turned to the Prince and resumed her social duties.

At this point, the quest for identification must stop. There is, for instance, little Nancy Cozens, aged eleven and a half, the author of *Bursting Ripe*, which, on the strength of Samuel Shodbutt's review, had sold twenty-five thousand on the day of publication. Of course we think of Daisy Ashford, whose *Young Visiters* had been introduced by Sir James Barrie. But *Young Visiters* was published in 1919, and Nancy Cozens is in no real way modelled on Daisy Ashford. Lewis was cramming into *The Roaring Queen*, set in 1930, all his observations of publishing gained in a lifetime of writing. But one sees how his mind worked, and it was the mind of the comic writer. The foil to Nancy Cozens is the four-times widowed, eighty-six-year-old Mrs Boniface, whose *Footsteps in the Sand* had won the Best First Novel of the Year award. The fact of the infant prodigy had bred, as it were, the notion of the senile prodigy.

Other characters, like Osorio Potter, seem to me to be like minor figures who have strayed out of Lewis' much more important satire on the arts, *The Apes of God*. *The Roaring Queen* has the role of a farcical footnote to that work, a footnote in which he takes satirical swipes at the trends in literature and society that he disapproves of, the cults of the detective novel, the tough Western, the homosexual novel, the youth cult, the Negro cult. All are summarily parodied; as too is the form of the novel itself, which is the Peacockian novel of Aldous Huxley.

As a novel, *The Roaring Queen* obviously has no great distinction. It is a *jeu d'esprit*, a squib, but it is authentic Lewis, and only he could have written it. It goes along at a spanking pace and it is very funny, not only as a cartoon of the book world of the day but, more precisely, as a caricature of one of its most famous inhabitants. Shodbutt is in character throughout, and in his rendering of him Lewis reaches considerable comic heights. Witness the scene in which Shodbutt and his wife discuss how he came to choose *It Takes Two to Make a Bedroom-Scene!* as the Book of the Week:

'It was the last line that decided me. It carried me off my feet.'
'Mine too!'
'The last line. On the last page. I said *This is the goods*. And I'm not often wrong. I could tell it at a glance.'
'There was one in the middle . . .'
'I remember that – I remember – you told me about it. A chapter full of genius, wasn't it? It must have been.'
'No, it was a line.'
'I remember it! It went deep – *a line only*. Marvellous. I never read the middle of a book. À quoi bon!'
'En effet!'
'Cela ne rîme à rien.'
'Tu as raison, cher S.S.'
'The middle of anything is *always* a bore. Even with such a book as *It Takes Two to Make a Bedroom-Scene*, it is a bore. The middle cannot be anything but a bore.'
'How I agree with you! There are very few books that bear reading in the middle. For me *c'est le premier pas qui coûte*.'
'Not for me – not for me! It all lies in *the last page*.'

'Of course, the last page . . .'

'I *never* read more than the last page. Balzac said he knew what a book was like without even opening it. I can't say that – that's more than I can claim – I take off my hat to Balzac! He was a *genius*! No. I have to *open* them. It's no use – I admit it, I have to open them. But I never need to go farther than the last page.'

'I know!'

'If that doesn't stir me, I just shut it up with a bang, and mark it N.G. But give me a last page – and I'm infallible. Infallible.'

'You would be infallible even if you never opened . . .'

'No, no. Balzac – *Balzac*! Not me! I take off my hat to Balzac! I must *open* it!

'You do yourself an injustice.'

'No. I can't tell if a book has genius unless I open it. No, Joanie – not without opening it!'

'But Sam, darling, often you *haven't*. It has been sufficient for me to *tell* you, in a nutshell . . .'

'That is true. Nutshell. Yes!'

'It is perfectly marvellous the way *the slightest hint* – why one word sometimes is enough. I have known you to decide upon the title alone!'

'That is true, yes. There have been times. I have often done that. A title – I *have* done it with only the title. But that's risky, Joanie! Risky!'

'I think your *flair* is unbelievable! I am positive that if I told Balzac the little that I have sometimes told *you*, he would never have been able to judge unerringly – to judge as you have always done. Not even Flaubert could!'

'Ah, *Flaubert*! I take off my hat to Flaubert! Flaubert was a genius! He would have told at once – even if the book had never been written.'

'I believe he could! But so could you – you know you could, S.S.!'

There, it seems to me, we can see unmistakably Lewis' affinities as a comic writer with Dickens and Ben Jonson.

WALTER ALLEN

23

CHAPTER 1

WHOSE was that imposing bust, worthy of Spy (button-holed and adipose-lined from Georgian state-banquets), making its lordly way down the Paddington platform? Whose majestic profiled upholstered *embonpoint* was it that blocked for a spell the Pullman corridor – whose hand could it be that had flung the rich travelling rug upon the first-class corner seat with that gesture – whose mass that then returned arrogantly to obstruct the corridor? Whose but Shodbutt's? Who was this but Samuel Shodbutt himself! It could be none other, and there with him almost at his heels was Mrs S.S.

With appropriate fuss the courteous ten-thirty, panting and with some proud snorts, as of a self-conscious charger (bestrid by a world-beating generalissimo), left the station. At one of its windows, grim and calm, could be discerned the progressive bust (moving on its way with stateliness, conferring lustre upon the entire ten-thirty) of the almighty Shodbutt. Loftily he stared out, and he saw giant posters cravenly soliciting his custom for Craven A, there was Mr Drage craftily and kindly eyeing Mr Everyman, there were the bold brews of Buchanan and of Bass, lounge suits of Moss and the glosses of Combinol, the bodies of Daimlers and Dunlop's road-hogging non-skidders, the hotels of the Dee, Don and Spey, the baths of Baden-Baden. And S.S. swept past each and all with napoleonic indifference, in the stately ten-thirty.

Samuel Shodbutt faced the engine and Mrs S.S. faced the

guard's van. As befitted a Lord of Alphabets *en voyage* (we all understand French here? but if not *tant pis!* for we shall be much in Shodbutt's company – it is essential) S.S. sat bolt upright. He was bound for the Oxfordshire borough of Bummenden, and beyond that for the seat of the Wellesley-Crooks – he had his week-end outfit of a fat old dandy in his bulging suitcases, groaning within the racks. There was his secretary – not a wife, not a money-mate, or a love-mate, but a useful Modern Woman – Joan Salford that was first, now Mrs S.S. Whereas S.S. weltered, cosily and grandly, in the vale of years, Mrs S.S. was only half-way down her little hill. His third partner. A magnate with a small sensible non-luxury car, that was S.S. with his latest youngish Old Dutch of a stenographer – business bed-partners, both sleeping, of the flourishing firm of Samuel Shodbutt – S.S. for short – a contented couple. Books *can* be Big Business, they can that, if properly handled! Books can be The Goods!

A mile out of Paddington an express train hit them with a vicious smack. There it clung, clapper-clapper for some clamorous seconds. It was chock-a-block. Its shuttle clapping in and out and up and down, it clung violently to them, weaving a cacophonous kaleidoscope, with a great din. It was a higher train than their train. Perhaps it was the Flying Scotsman himself. But Shodbutt would know this as a matter of course. Crossly its crazy cinema was watched – Shodbutt eyed it with that frown he gave all things of that sort. But as one of its quick crooked pictures flashed up, clicked and crashed, knocked out by the next, Samuel S. looked thoughtful.

'I know that face!'

S.S. not only *thought* – that was not his way – he *said* it. What he knew he knew, there was no getting away from it and with him to *know* was to *say*, and *he knew that face*, and there was no reason why you should not know that he knew. With nail-driving emphasis, with the grim snarl of his home-town, it was rapped out, in a nasty staccato. Adenoids accounted for some of it, yes: but Snekkheaton-over-Pegpot was the smoky birth-place of that slow nasal high-pitched snarl. There, in Snekkheaton-over-Pegpot, competition (for little Shodbutts born there) was keen. Under the shadow of booming Victorian industries man was pressed close up against man. There was no room for 'the Graces' between the loom and the lathe. The voice learnt to snarl young – to stutter and answer back.

'I know that face! Where have I seen it?' Samuel Shodbutt stuttered again. And his wife facing the guard's van (past which the guard of the express flashed and was gone with a parting bang) said 'Whose, darling?' for at first she had thought S.S. was composing his next Monday's blurb for the B.O.T.W.C.'s circular merely.

'I believe it was young Wooley sitting in that compartment!'

For Shodbutt railway trains were made up of 'compartments', for with French railways that·was the case and Shodbutt was one travelled man – before now he had been mistaken at the first blush by Frenchmen for a Gascon bagman with a cold in the head.

'Which compartment, darling?' Mrs S.S. inquired.

'In the third coach!' said Samuel Shodbutt, picking a tooth, the last to lose its nerve, with leisurely tongue-suction, the celebrated receding chin taking on its typical puckers. He but just suppressed that habit of cocky young days in Snekkheaton-under-Pegpot, that is to puncture the air with a smart kiss, to show that the tooth is *picked*; or musically to extract a last moist morsel.

'I didn't see any coaches,' said Joanie.

'No?'

'No, darling. You don't mean in that express train that just passed?'

'Yes. In that train that just passed!'

'Oh but that went past too *quickly* for me to be able to see anyone sitting in one of its *coaches*!'

Samuel Shodbutt was silent. He continued, with puckered chin and mouth hitched up at one corner, to threaten to make that cocky noise, while he sent a puzzled frown into the distance.

'Was it young Wooley . . . ?' King Shodbutt spoke to himself (even as the Cabots speak only with God).

'What is that, darling?'

'Who got it the last week in June last year — with his *Red Cloud over Cub*?'

'No, darling, that was David Bronowski I think. Yes that was David Bronowski I am sure.'

'Wooley! Wooley I think — am I right? Yes. It was *Wooley*!'

'Wooley was the second week in September, darling. He got it with *Don't Care was Made to Care*!'

'No, Joanie, no! Wooley! It was Wooley. *Don't Care was Made to Care*! A fine book that — a deep book! — a deep thing! *Depth — depth*!'

Samuel half-closed his crossly-drowsy eyes, and, every inch the holiday-watercolourist, limned the air with two fat pontifical fingers, above *depths* at which the mind grew dizzy — the chiaroscuro as it were of the mysterious deeps of genius.

'A deep book, Joanie. A deep book!'

'Yes it was a good book,' said Joanie. 'I liked *Don't Care was Made to Care*!'

'More than that it was a *great* book!' crashed S.S.

'Perhaps — even a *great* book!'

Another express train hit them with a smack. One damned thing after another! Samuel S. frowned.

'Well anyhow,' then snarled S.S., when this second express had let go and banged off into thin air, 'I wish *I'd* written the damned book, that's all I can say!'

Joanie gave Samuel the sweet underlook that said *You are so generous, darling S.S. Everyone knows that!* and lowered her eyes again.

And for ten minutes Mr Samuel Shodbutt sat bolt upright facing the engine frowning. Upon his left knee he clutched *The Idiot* (Dostoevski) and upon his right he balanced *The Thirteenth Commandment* – the Book of the Week Club's choice for the week before last.

Samuel Shodbutt's richly-tailored *embonpoint* was regal. Literature was the richer for Samuel Shodbutt's appearance, and S.S. was the richer for Literature. A lock of sallow leaden silver oppressed his right-hand temple – he had the constant frown of Power – the frown of the Power-of-the-pen – to make and to mar, of course: the great critic's frown *in excelsis*. For this was a Literary Emperor. Or was not Shodbutt the dream of a literary emperor (or of a French literary pontiff) by a mid-Victorian haberdasher?

Samuel Shodbutt was indeed just a *dream-come-true*. He was the haberdasher, he was the haberdashery, he was the dream of the haberdasher. He was even that self-made Potentate of the Pen, as conceived by a conceited mid-Victorian haberdasher – *climbed up and proud of it!*

Then S.S.'s latter days were dream-like too, never quite sure was he at all whether the express was going or coming – was this week's or last week's indeed! The weekly figures in his Book-of-the-Week World came and went with such staggering rapidity. At last he had his purple place (the place that was a purple patch) in the full purple beams of the literary sun. A Canute of 1930 he sat upon the verge of a journalist puddle, and he quelled it with his frowning eye. From its dismal surface, each fresh week, a new sun shone, of burning 'genius' – and these luminaries were the selected Stars, picked more or less at hazard (often by Joanie) from the pullulating 'geniuses' vouched for in each new announcement by the various publishing houses.

Shodbutt lifted up his stately blackcorseted bust, cast as it were for the mid-Victorian haberdasher in black and green chocolate, and he spoke as follows:

'Joanie!' he said. 'Did you notice as we came along the passage – did you notice Joyce Bishop?'

Joanie had seen their colleague of the *Sunday Eyeball*, as they came along the passage, in spite of herself she had been made aware of the presence of Joyce Bishop.

'I wonder if she's going there too?' Shodbutt's brow and chin were both now furrowed.

'It looks like it.' And Joan expressed her dislike of Mrs Bishop by a frown after the pattern of that of Samuel but in pale porcelain.

'What a woman,' said S.S. '*What* a woman.'

'Indeed you are right,' said Joan. 'But I prefer her to Marjorie Plunkett.'

The great man ploughed up his chin in scorn, and shrugged his shoulders.

'Il y a fagots et fagots,' he said. He shrugged again, as French as French.

'That is true,' said Joan. 'But Marjorie is the world's fagot!'

'I thought I caught sight,' Samuel spoke again, 'as we got out of the taxi, of old Jermingham. I was possibly mistaken.'

'Matey?' asked Joan, and she showed, by the slight toning down of her brightness, how very distasteful she would regard an encounter with 'Matey'.

'The same,' said S.S. 'Matey. Yes. I lost sight of him. But I believe he was making for our train.'

'If *he* is to be there, I suggest we return tomorrow the first thing in the morning.'

'That's just what I was thinking,' the great man rejoined; and he tossed his lead-white curl, and furrowed up his chin that fell away into the winged collar.

When the Shodbutts descended at Bummenden, they immediately discerned 'Matey' alighting at the other extremity of the train. 'Matey' was the big noise of the *Fiction Belt* as it was facetiously called (this was the seasonal award for Non-Detective Fiction), and his big bellicose chin and portentous spectacles were unmistakably there, and not far from him sure enough was Joyce Bishop ('il y a fagots et fagots') – they were making signals to each other. And there were many more besides.

Handing his suitcases to a porter and directing that they should be placed in the Wellesley-Crooks' car awaiting their arrival, S.S. hastened to the exit, to escape 'Matey', and in a lesser but sufficiently savage degree Joyce Bishop. To occupy the same Rolls-Royce as those two personalities – no, that was more than he was prepared to do – Shanks's Mare was preferable, and Shanks's Mare it should be! And Mr and Mrs Samuel Shodbutt set out on foot for the Wellesley-Crooks' country-house, S.S. swollen with understandable indignation. Neither he nor Joan uttered a word. You may live by words – you may live *fatly* by the word of your mouth, you may even enslave historic nations by the spoken word. But there are times when the words will fail you whoever you are, all the same. Such an occasion had now arisen: and Mr and Mrs S.S. directed their measured steps to the not far distant estate of the hospitable Crooks. Yes, this decidedly was to be *the* most awful party. Shodbutt as never before was on his mettle: he would give the

Wellesley-Crooks the biggest piece of his mind he had ever yet parted with at one breath, and that before the morning was much older.

CHAPTER 2

At the precise moment, when, like any Good Companion or Merry Good Fellow, Samuel Shodbutt took the road (rather than travel in the Wellesley-Crooks' buses with the rest of the Book-World – who need never have been asked – was not the president of the Book of the Week Club enough? – why this *embarras de richesse?*), at that moment precisely the Honourable Baby Bucktrout strolled into the Tool House up at Beverley Chase, not above a kilometre as the crow flies from where Shodbutt stalked. She was clothed only in white tennis-shorts and a polo-singlet of the same Sienna sun-tan complexion as her skin, while she sucked in her lean cheeks without thinking, to enhance the attractive hatchet-lines of her close Eton crop. She was a pocket-amazon, for she stood no more than five feet high in her sandalled feet and was of an airy build.

The Tool House was dark, it smelt of damp turf, and the sweetish sweat of uncouth males (i.e. of the Beverley Chase gardeners), and Poor Tom, the youngest and cheapest of the outdoor staff, who was a local eighteen-year-old, Oxfordshire-bred and born, was there hiding his sweetness behind a large lawn-mower, which he was engaged in oiling.

Poor Tom was always to be found there about that time, oiling or sharpening something. And Baby Bucktrout knew it! (You can readily imagine what this means – I need not employ a second exclamation mark – it was the way of a maid with a man, or the way of a pocket-amazon with a huge and vegetative agriculturist.)

Baby took up a lubricating tin which crackled beneath her podgy fingers, and she fixed its tin neck against another grass-mower and directed the grateful fluid in turn to the cranks of a flotilla of lawn-mowers.

'Well, Tom,' said Baby, as she squeezed the oil-laden belly of the lubricating tin. 'Well, Tom. I said "Well" – Tom!'

Well! Poor Tom blushed, up to the roots of his ginger locks, and persevered with his trade as it was his duty to do, filling the machine with far more mobiloil, however, than it needed for the closest crop for the most velvet turf of the most posh family seat.

'Poor Tom!' said Baby. 'May I call you Poor Tom? You sweet lamb! *Poor* Tom!'

Tom trembled in every limb and absorbed himself in his lowly occupation, hoping that a little chivalry might be generated in the bosom of his hard-boiled mistress at the spectacle of such a busy boy.

But the Hon. Baby Bucktrout strolled over to Poor Tom and stroked the perspiring ginger locks. She lifted a great dripping tongue of hair, of a carroty sunset complexion, and hung it up on his left ear, to be tidy only. Squatting upon his cart-horse haunches Poor Tom redoubled his manual activities – he removed the perforated swivel-collar from the lawn-sprinkler and began to blow into it for dear life.

'May I ask you something, Tom darling?' asked Baby.

And, grimly blowing, Tom bent his head lower, over the sprinkler, with a deep ginger blush.

Accustomed to the unrestrained smells of the most exotic plants, in the atmospheres of the hottest greenhouses, Poor Tom nevertheless felt absolutely queasy as his nostrils admitted the aroma of the brand-new Coty purchased on purpose by Baby to appeal to the so-far impervious snout of this sodden horticulturist: but *this* stuff, it was at once evident,

33

penetrated his blood-stream, setting up in very truth a furious heart-beat in the plucky lad, how should it not be so? Finally his body was convulsed, as he crouched at her feet, and unexpectedly was torn with a volcanic sneeze, of great voltage. The shed shook.

'Oh! Your health – God keep you!' Baby exclaimed with a deep-seated sneer of dominant budding womanhood. And not realizing of course that she had given him a dose of hay-fever with her *Quelques Fleurs*, she approached still nearer and casually took her seat, as if he had been an untame but sluggish nag, upon his brawny ox-like Oxfordshire back. Seizing the shrinking mammoth round the throat with her bare arms, she fastened herself upon him with equestrian matter-of-factness. Laying her head upon his shoulder but behind of course, she whispered in his ear:

'Tom, honey! Does it make you feel *queer* – does it, or does it not, make you feel queer, dear?'

She listened: there was no sound but expulsion and insuck of air into Tom's windpipe. 'Having me pick-a-back, Tom my treasure, must make you feel queer, dear!'

Tom struggled to rise, if he might, in dismay; but a deferential mount and true, in such a manner as not to spill the Honourable Baby.

'Do give me a ride, Tom – oh be a sport, Tom! Gallop me round the shed just once, kicking your heels up like mad, will you?'

Tom cautiously moved towards the perpendicular another inch or two.

'Am I too heavy, Tom? I'm *not*, you're foxing! You may ride me if you want to, turn and turn about! What do you say?'

Tom said nothing. All a-tremble, but as cautious as possible, slowly he straightened: gingerly he rose up, in mortal terror, then stood all a-flutter upright, upon his

34

carthorse corduroy-understandings. Poor Tom – he was indeed at bay!

'Why are you trembling, Tom?'

This tactless question made him shiver twice as much as before.

'Please catch hold of my legs this minute or I shall fall down and hurt myself!'

Poor Tom stood in his traces holding his breath like a twenty-fathom-man in the oyster-beds, not knowing which way to look or what to do. Between the freckled clefts of his cuirass of brawn sprouted the wet red hair, tinted like that upon head and hands, and each follicle was a little fountain. This was principally from shame, though the deference of his cautious movements, as he half-crouched, half-stood, imposed a strain upon the spirited yokel that accounted for more than a drop. But as he was what in oxen is called Dutch-buttocked – in short of a cloddy and capacious seat – this was not so difficult for him as it would have been had Tom been top-heavy and a less muscular lad in the middle.

Baby panted and clung above at not far short of an angle of forty-five, holding on.

'If you won't hold me, Tom,' she lisped upon his slippery neck, 'I must catch hold of something or I shall slip off.'

His trapezius was handy and she seized it.

'Gee up, Tom! Is the man having a nap or what? I believe, Tom, you are only a pack-mule after all. To look at, one would say you were a proper stud animal but you're not. You're only a beast of burden. You seem to think you're loaded up with saddle-bags instead of Me! We can't stand here for ever.'

Tom trembled at these harsh words.

'You great bloodshot lad,' the Baby hissed, 'where is your spirit?'

At the sound of this *foul language* so near to his ear the

35

'bloodshot lad' started as if he had been struck, for Tom wore his chapel-training upon his sleeve: but by this time the wretched young Goliath was tipsy with the perfumes of this polo-vested jockey of high degree. Resist the thought as he would, the fact of the sex of this soft steeple-chaser filled Tom's cerebellum with hell-fire. He felt himself *changing*, it was no use; could it be he was taking *that* road – was he not God-fearing? He trembled again as he thought of it. Beneath the horrid weight of her lascivious horsemanship was he in some way breaking down, or breaking up? Lacka-day! Tom was at present scarcely better than a centaur from the chest down, and that was a fact. Already the Enemy held all his leg-arches – his waistline and his Dutch-buttocks. The Tempter was entrenched in the lower reaches of his spine. Beelzebub had him round the waist, he must now disown all of himself below that plimsoll.

Gasping, half-choked with words of apology that would not materialize, Poor Tom made resolutely for the door, in a last despairing bolt to escape the defeat of his higher ego by the Powers of Darkness.

But Baby Bucktrout (for this was not the first time she had mounted Poor Tom) knew his weak spot. Brandishing her fingers in the air, she fastened them upon a spot betwixt two ribs, not far from the yokel's spleen. The effect was astonishingly instantaneous. Immediately he wheeled, doubled-up, bellowed and fell – almost flattening-out Miss Bucktrout as he crashed down in the fashion of a pole-axed ox; robbed of the last of his poor wits beneath the mad tickling attack of the electric fingers.

But Baby screamed with the raucous happiness of her sex at odds with man and clung to Tom like grim death. She attacked, one after the other, all his weak spots in turn, sending him into repeated convulsions. With great bellows of panic of a lost soul on its beam ends, the luckless Tom chased her hands about his electrified torso, wrenching them out of this place and dragging them off of that.

'Oh Tom, you wouldn't gallop!' hoarsely chuckled Baby, 'you're galloping now though, upside-down. You're more like a fish than a mammal really.'

And the great stupid lad bounded about on the floor like a Chinese cracker or a dragon on its back, outmatched by some Moon-maiden.

But at this point the Tool House was filled with the indignant accents of a roaring voice. Two powerful hands handcuffed her busy wrists, and Baby Bucktrout was seized by the waist and shoulders, and dragged squeaking and spitting off this man-in-a-fit, who in his convulsions was striking out right and left and had already damaged the most spectacular lawn-sprinkler up at Beverley Chase at all.

'How often shall I have to tell you, Miss Baby, to leave the men alone at their work, I should like to know!' the voice boomed in the shed.

'How dare you treat me like this!' the Baby bellowed back. 'I shall get you the sack tomorrow. Either *you* leave or *I* shall!'

'It would be better if you *did* go, Miss Baby – far better, it really would, where they can keep you in order in Oxford.'

'I *shall* go! I am not going to be treated like this! I will not stop an hour longer!'

'You ought to be ashamed of yourself, at your age, you should!'

'You old beast! You old worm! You Cossack!'

Baby left the Tool House kicking and biting, beneath Miss Corse's beefy arm. Baby knew Miss Corse's person by heart – and she knew that, unlike Poor Tom, Miss Corse had no weak spots whatever. She was not, in short, ticklish, nor susceptible at all to pain – for there was scarcely any part of Miss Corse that at one time or another Baby Bucktrout had not scratched or bitten, it was phenomenal what punishment Corse could take.

'I shall tell her ladyship that if she *will* allow you to be given books to read like that there Lawrence's – yes, you know what I mean well enough.'

'No I don't, you horrible devil. . .'

'*Lady Chatterley's Lover.*'

'You old liar – I never read it – I daresay you have though!' came from under the arm, which received a fresh bite.

'I daresay I have! Yes, *I* had a look at it, never you fear, my fine young lady! *There's* a nice book for young ladies to be given! I only wish I could meet the dirty filthy man that wrote it and tell him what I thought of him!'

And Miss Corse strode towards the house, exclaiming as she went: 'I'm sure I don't know what they teach you at Oxford!'

And Baby wept and kicked, watched by two footmen from behind a shrubbery, attracted by the uproar; and Poor Tom lay panting upon the earthen floor of the Tool House, his fists in the air and his mouth open, from which two words issued:

'Great guns!'

It was his daddy's favourite expression.

CHAPTER 3

Now some hours before the unfolding of these ill-assorted events – namely that of the outrage upon Poor Tom in the Tool House, and that of the stormy arrival of the bookish tide upon the quiet platforms of Bummenden in Oxfordshire, and of the Shodbutts' glowering route-march upwards, bearing down in high dudgeon upon the princely lodges of Beverley Chase – a few hours prior to these ill-assorted to-dos – a young man got out of bed in London. A young Star, featuring in this simple narrative, got out of a great London four-poster, built to accommodate half a dozen Test Match tourists, as it was opposite the Midland Terminus, or else a couple of outsize love-birds as the case might be – for this was one in a considerable block of indelicate hotels, well known for not being particular.

Much as we may hate to thrust our way backwards through eventful Time, which, like the equally clockwork Tide, waits for no man, much less us – dense with momentous accidents – in order to relate this earlier occurrence, it must be done. Go back we must, for this young man's levee is for us an event. Not as great an event – how could it be? – as Shodbutt's departure from Paddington Station in the historic ten-thirty, and therefore not to be given precedence over that capital item, no: yet a matter of some moment. We *have* to go back. We are swimming against the time-tide, it is understood, against the time-table, even. But we will be breathless and brief. We will not suspend the Book-World for too long without the portals of the Wellesley-

Crooks' estate – they shall get in after a very insignificant delay!

Nine-thirty struck in the mock middle-Gothic turret of Holy Trinity, Bishops Road. The young man in question crashed out of bed, in muscular eruption, and began fiercely treading the floor of the hotel bedroom, yawning like the Metro-Goldwyn lion itself which precedes the play, giving forth its hollow roar. He bound up his index finger which had begun to bleed again. He had cut it with a paper-knife and the fingerstall had left his finger while he slept, so the cicatrice had opened. That's what came of reading rotten prize-verse, bitterly he reflected as he slipped on his Oxford bags, or at all events his dirty trousers, and lit a Lucky Strike. Such were the fruits of too great inquisitiveness where other people's verses were concerned – and what verses! That is what came of a lack of self-control. For why should he have bought that booklet with its paper-band announcing it as 'The Choice of the Hopkins Club for the Spring's Best Book of Verse', every third page of which had to be raped with some sharp instrument?

He went over and shook a sleeping figure in another hefty bedstead. A curse rose upon the grim and comfortless air of the great London bedchamber, an automatic epithet of moderate wrath.

'Get up, you besotted cop, firebrand and early bird!' roughly he shouted, looking very tough and attractive.

A second curse ascended from the second bed, urged through jaws still mortised in slumber.

'Call yourself a detective!' he exclaimed with a gruelling contempt. 'I could commit half a dozen fresh homicides while you were investigating the first, if I were your quarry. I should ask nothing better than to have *you* on my track, Charlie!'

There was a rumble of deep discontent.

'The sleeping sleuth!' he sneered. 'Behold our sleeping sleuth!'

A third, a very bitter curse, came from the occupant of the second bed, who was becoming personal – he was waking up.

'Very well,' said the young bravo, as he strode (like a he-man from Hollywood, half-stripped for the Box Office, muscling-in upon the female majority) towards the hot-and-cold water, seized a tarnished starfish tap. 'Sleep the sleep of *the just*, you beastly policeman! I'm off to Bummenden, you can pay the bill! Good luck!'

A clap of coarse laughter broke from the occupied bed. But a few minutes later the door slammed and the double-bedded Paddington hotel-room only held one person; but that person was now struggling up from the tortured blankets of the second four-poster and revealed himself as a very fat young man with a placidly worried mastiff-like countenance, dourly-dewlapped and with wrinkled brows, a couple of dark dissipated bags beneath lacklustre eyes, and a ragged blondish hedge of bristling stalks above the ploughed field of his forehead. From under this forked hedge he stared at nothing in particular – a ponderous imp embedded in a hay-loft, heaving with a dogged hiccup. He massaged his big plump face, blinked with deliberation, hiccupped again, ran his dry tongue around inside his lips, and was on his feet – the flabby body mobilized in the twinkling of an eye – and was scratching his way over sluggishly towards the bottle-green blind, which he shot up with a wallop without looking, still scratching. He then surveyed his ravaged youth in the looking-glass – he saw it steadily and he saw it whole. He eyed it with a noble im-passivity. Then he proceeded to wash off lazily the stains of the night, and dried his face cautiously upon the hotel-towel, which had an effete human smell of the dried spindrift of cheap soap.

'So!' he muttered darkly. 'So!' Three hangovers in as many days! *The Sleeping Sleuth!* Ah well! He shaved. To shave a mastiff cannot be an easy task but he had had much practice. He scrubbed at his discoloured teeth without hope of dispersing the unlovely tartar; but he never more than half-smiled with a stranger, for he realized that this was no advertisement. His long suit, as he saw it, was the wistful moroseness of his face. He was a big fat unhappy dog but faithful unto death. Or so he read the message to the world of a rather difficult physique to handle.

Reunited over ham and eggs in the coffee-room, these two room-mates considered the prospect of the ramped entrance of the terminus, down which they were able to observe the beluggaged cabs disappearing as they came from Spring Street or from Praed Street, under the inhospitable flank of the terminus-hotel.

'How is your finger, Ossie?' asked the fat young man, indifferently drawling, a sallow eye upon his egg. 'You must have been uncommonly tight to wound yourself with a paper-knife.'

'Do you think so?'

'You were flourishing it about like a dervish, I seem to recollect, as you cut the leaves of your book of poetry. It was poetry, wasn't it?'

'I really couldn't say.'

'It looked as if you meant to slice up the bally thing. You hate poetry, don't you?'

'Some people's.'

'Other people's. But I think you must be careful of edged tools. Also listen – take more water with it, if you'll allow me to say so. Take my advice as an older man.'

Ossie gave a sour sneer, but held his peace.

'You'll get yourself jugged one of these days, mark my words if you don't.'

Ossie scowled.

'As a policeman . . .' he began to retort.

'As a private inquiry agent, please,' the fat young man corrected him.

'As a policeman, I said. As a policeman everything with you leads to the lock-up.'

The fat young man sighed.

'My profession has brought home to me the unpalatable fact that almost everything can get you into gaol, if persisted in long enough – even the detection of crime is no exception.'

'I'm glad that at last you realize the true nature of your calling.'

'Oh, the private inquiry agent is always skating on thin ice.'

'Very, I should think.'

'Half the time he's exposing himself to criminal proceedings, as housebreaker or what not. There's no getting away from that.'

'All policemen are crooked,' Ossie exclaimed with a fine boyish dogmatism blazing from his sultry eyes, accustomed to brood over the 'mysteries' of Crime Clubs, the central figures of which were corpses – as in the 'sad stories' of the early English kings, '*all murdered*'. He was one of your black Britons, both in eye and hair. He brought a fire to British-ness that is wanting in the Saxon blood. It was an unintelligent fire of course, it conformed to the Saxon leaven.

'Not all,' his fat friend demurred. '*Not all.*'

'Yes, all. Crooks.' He smiled, with a sulky approval of his own dogmatism. 'Crooks!' he crowed savagely. 'Crooks!' he crowed again.

His well-covered friend put on a pipe – as the Coffee Room would describe it. When he had first turned sleuth, after the tedium of Oxford, this fat young man had purchased his meerschaum and his briar, and any criminal could scent him a mile off on account of his particular blend of back-block baccy — without which of course he was lost.

'You are thinking of *foreign* policemen, Ossie,' he said, inflating his smoke-filled cheeks like some Gothic Aeolus, and sending a cloud across the breakfast table, to climb the shoulders of the aggressive Ossie, exhaling the pungency of tropical colonies.

'No, all policemen. They are murderers!' The laconic Ossie stuck to his sawed-off shotguns of Chicago romance — nodding his head at each abrupt statement of stolid dogma, as if to throw each handful of vocables down to trump and trump again, playful and truculent. 'Murderers!' he nodded again with great energy. Almost a wink burst from this heavy-handed young teaser, except that both eyelids dropped at once.

'You have been reading the *Daily Worker* — you mean they are "murderers" because they club the Unemployed, is that it? I seem to have heard "murderer" before, shouted by some drab *tricoteuse* from the ranks of a hunger-march at a passing troop of mounted police, in Birmingham maybe.'

'No, that's their duty.'

'Oh!'

'Of course it is. That is nothing — hunger-marchers are a bore.'

'Nothing? But on the continent perhaps the cops *do* merit the capital charge. The Sûreté Général, now, the French C.I.D., you know. They, *we know*, stick at nothing: they are the *Cheka* of the Third Republic — in its last phase of bourgeois bolshevism.'

'Why should they? We don't. Why should they!'

'I didn't say they shouldn't. Murder to them admittedly

is a bagatelle. They bump off anybody they are asked to by their omnipotent masonic bosses and patrons.'

'What is *masonic* – isn't it something old men dress up and do, with trowels and aprons, silly old fools?'

'Oh, it is nothing much here – a very expensive club, with countersigns and druid investitures, that's all. Quite respectable.'

'Is it religious – like the Quakers?'

'It's a little bag of tricks imported from the Ancient East – since Goths and Germans are not good apparently at thinking up such things and so fell for them in the superstitious ages. Same dope the crooked Templars picked up in the Holy Land – have you heard of that lot? A crazy bunch of half-baked savages, "strong i' the arm and weak i' the head"!'

'Were they Yorkshiremen?'

'Not all. But the old dope works marvels still in some places. We were talking of France. *There* it positively turns the public services of law and order into a tale of Ali Baba and the Forty Thugs – a sort of blood and thunder pantomime. You can't get on in the Sûreté at all if you aren't a mason, so old Daudet says.'

'Who is Daudet?'

'Oh, he is a ridiculous royalist. But he knows his France inside-out: he has lived outside the system of the Third Republic all his life and has made it his business of course to show it up. What he doesn't know is not worth knowing.'

'I can't read French.'

'Well, you ought to. You are neglecting your education for detective fiction. You'd get a lot of fun out of French.'

'I don't know what you're talking about, anyway.'

'You should pay more attention to fact and less to fiction. Truth is stranger than fiction – Shakespeare said it.'

'The French are not the only crooks, if you're saying they're crooks – I suppose you are.'

'French society is very corrupt; and incredibly masonic – in the underworld at the top. In the *richissime* underworld at the top of that tumbledown old pyramid. Rotten to the tip.'

'They are just the same here.'

'Oh no, you are quite wrong. Not a bit of it. It is very different. They are not mystical and masonic, to start with. Scotland Yard is not a Mafia, all said and done. It is a respectable machine for the detection of crime.'

'There is no policeman anywhere who cannot be bought,' Ossie thundered, looking daggers at his bland, fat friend, whom he suspected of having handcuffs in his pocket.

'You are thinking of America probably, through the medium of gangster literature.'

'No, not America. Here.'

'In America of course the police are bought by the bunch. Police, politician and gunman make one big barefaced racket. And in France the Sûreté is the most efficient, trustworthy and reliable murder-gang available, on French soil – provided you possess the correct masonic password or sign to set the machine in motion. French big-business is mystic and masonic, that accounts for what happens there. But not here, Ossie. We are a dull, straight lot – we are a terribly straight lot.'

He wagged his head broodingly over the straightness prevailing in Great Britain, and extending even here and there to the Colonies.

'Rot!' Ossie barked. 'We're worse than the Frogs because we're hypocrites!'

'Oh, that!'

'We're a bunch of sanctimonious crooks!'

'No, we are not even that. We have no Grand Orient, we have no Tammany. We have no dacoits. We do *not* take money to tie people down to railway-lines for ritualist decapitation, and on the principle that dead men tell no tales.'

'Yes we do!'

'I beg your pardon, we do not.'

'So you say.'

'Would our criminal police undertake a political murder, even if the Minister of the Interior ordered it? They would not.'

'Of course they would,' Ossie contemptuously asserted. 'Of course they would.'

But Ossie was looking sideways at his friend out of one eye with growing suspicion and hostility.

'I wasn't talking about political crimes, I know nothing about that,' he said sullenly. 'What's politics got to do with it? Politics don't interest me.'

'Well, politics and money are so mixed up at this time that it is impossible to say where one leaves off and the other begins, you see. *The money-men have grown political.* And they have grown criminal. It's just the same, do you see, as that there is no straight "labour" issue. All industrial labour issues are political issues. And the money-men are converting their mere *money* into *power*. You can watch them doing it. It is very shrewd of them, since money pure and simple can't last much longer. So they have taken to the bomb and pistol, in countries less well organized than ours. Here they confine themselves to boycott.'

'You don't mention the ordinary sort of crime, I notice. You keep going off at a tangent. I'm talking of ordinary crime.'

'Not at all — all crime is ordinary.'

'Ordinary? Some is. But you're talking about the secret service. Everyone knows *they* put people on the spot. Read Somerset Maugham or Gordon Seton Hutchinson.'

The fat young man burst out laughing.

'Yes, read Maugham and Colonel Seton Hutchinson. *The Hairless Mexican!* That is good!'

'Well, isn't it true? Have you read *The Hairless Mexican*? I have.'

'Yes, I have. But you exaggerate the mere policeman's turpitude. Don't I know better than you do? Many detectives, over here, are extremely respectable men. Their palms are horny and unoiled. They are God-fearing fathers of families. They are church sidesmen – they lift up their voices in prayer.'

'So you say.'

'It's a fact. You would argue that just as the last thing a Harley Street specialist wishes to do is to *cure* anybody, so the last thing the police want to do is to stamp out crime.'

'Put it any way you like. All the crimes that are unaccounted for are the work of the police. Everybody knows that.'

'Not here.'

'I heard a man say so yesterday in Hyde Park. The police stood and listened. They wouldn't do that if it weren't true.'

'I know it sounds dull, but the British policeman . . .'

'Of course you are bound to say that! You are one of them.'

'I am a private inquiry agent. I secrete myself in cupboards, and seek to unloosen by foul means or fair the unholy bonds of matrimony that eat into the flesh of my deserving clients.'

'That's not all you do. How much, Charlie, would you ask to bump off somebody for me, now? I ask you in your professional capacity.'

'What are your resources, sir? I have described to you the conditions obtaining in England. It still requires more £sd to corrupt an Englishman than to corrupt a man of any other nationality. The Briton has kept up his price. Such things are not mixed up with mysticism or politics here.

Murder is still crime for us. And crime is very costly. For plain unvarnished "crime" you have to *pay*!'

'What's your price?'

'Every man has his price, and I am no exception to that rule. But I am an Englishman, remember that.'

'Name your figure, Charlie.'

'Do you want somebody bumped off? Who is it, lady or gent?'

'They are gents.'

'Members of the University?'

Ossie hesitated.

'One is.' He frowned – he had been led into an admission. 'Supposing *one* is, anyway, for argument's sake.'

'Undergraduates? Do they write novels? Ah, I see they do! You blush! I thought as much. It is in your capacity of "author", Ossie . . . !'

'Name your figure. And not so many questions!'

'I should have to know all the details first. It might be quite easy: or it might be the reverse. How can I say? It all depends.'

'You want to know too much.'

'Not at all – one job is quite different from another. But why don't you do it yourself?'

'I have my reasons.'

'It is cheaper, and I should have thought more satisfactory. I am sure you feel very strongly about it. You feel so strongly about everything. It would surely be a personal satisfaction to you that it should be your hand that dealt the blow. Why delegate it? Do your own dirty work, in other words, and keep your filthy lucre in your pocket.'

'Are you a professional man or not?'

'Certainly. That's just it.'

'You don't think I've got the dough, I can see what it is!'

The fat young man drew himself up, and gave his

would-be client a haughty professional stare, his brow very wrinkled, his eyes drooping very much at the outer extremities.

'I'm afraid it's not very much in our line, to be frank, Mr Potter,' he said with dignity. 'Not much in our line, really, you see. We *do*, it is true, for clients of long and honourable standing, occasionally undertake such matters. But we don't like it: we don't really care for it! There it is. As Englishmen we experience a natural distaste, if you understand me, for these rather messy transactions. No, sir, I am sorry: I think you would do well, under the circumstances, to consult someone else.' The fat young man rose in the stately fashion of the fat, thrust his hands beneath his jacket where it stuck out at the rear, and stood gazing down upon his scowling fellow-player. 'We can of course supply you with the address of several very – er – capable firms, to whom you could take your proposal and I daresay they would consider it. We don't really touch that end of the business. We prefer not to. It is a rule of our house. I am sorry, Mr Potter, but there it is!'

Ossie rose with great abruptness, his chair falling backwards violently, as he did so.

'You're a blackguard, Charlie, and you know it!' he shouted.

Charlie bowed.

'At your service, Mr Potter!'

'It is only because you think I haven't got the dough.'

'No, really! No, really not!'

'It's your *job* after all!'

Charlie turned himself into the heavy professional paterfamilias: he placed a hand upon the shoulder of his 'young friend'.

'You are too romantic, Ossie,' he exclaimed with a fruity geniality. 'Much too romantic. If I were a Frenchman, now, or a Yank! We *do* draw the line! We do really – we have to. We are, after all, British.'

'Well, I'll take my order elsewhere.'

'It is as you please, my dear Mr Potter.'

'But if you think you've convinced me that you are not a murderer you're very much mistaken!'

Charlie interrupted him with a gesture of deprecation that Ossie should regard him as so short-sighted.

'I've just been reading a book,' Ossie went on, 'where one of your fraternity arranged a slap-up murder, *in the smallest detail . . .!*'

'Yes! "In the smallest detail"?'

'For *a man they'd never clapped eyes on before.*'

'You don't say so!'

'And we are *friends*! Or *supposed* to be!' Ossie was very withering as he added this.

'Was it a Crime Club?' asked Charlie with a winning melancholy smile.

'No. It was *not* a Crime Club. As a matter of fact it was by an undergraduate.'

'Ah, well you're a confiding sort of fellow. Do you know what's the matter with you? You are too susceptible to the printed word. Yours is a case of advanced *Bovarysme* too. You are so romantic you will never be happy until you've gone to gaol!'

'Good old policeman!' Ossie looked up at the clock above the mantelpiece. 'I shall miss the train. It is ten twenty-five.'

'When does it go?'

'Ten-thirty.'

'Then you have missed it already.'

But Ossie rushed to the door, the fat young man following him, pressing the electric bell as he passed it.

'I will see you off,' he called. 'I have to buy a paper in the station.'

51

Four minutes and fifty seconds later they were bowling down the ramp to the Booking Offices. The train had left when they burst out upon the platform.

'You are romantic about Time, too, you see,' said the fat young man softly, bending an eye of gentle banter upon him. 'The clock's the clock! It doesn't slow down for you to catch trains.'

'I shouldn't have missed it if you hadn't stopped to get change!' said Ossie. 'Why get change?'

'You are romantic about money too!'

But on this head Ossie held his tongue.

'I am *not*, however, I am afraid,' his fat friend told him. 'You owe me five and sixpence on that bill, young man.'

Ossie counted out the money in contemptuous silence, coin by coin, into the other's 'unromantic' palm.

The next train, somewhat slower, left in twenty minutes. As they passed the bookstall, on the way to the Refreshment Saloon, the young detective stopped, and sang the word *Gringoire* across the counter, but received a shake of the head from Smith and Son, who responded to his musical inquiry with a flat *Matin*, followed by a sotto voce *Journal*, and he flung down fourpence on top of a *Vogue* and accepted the latter.

'*Le Journal*,' he muttered contemptuously to his indifferent companion who had no French and didn't want any. 'If I can't get a good newspaper I get a bad one,' and he flourished what he had bought.

'Why is that? Why buy any? I never do, except the *News of the World*.'

'It is my system. If I can't get a good one – and the good ones are usually not stocked – I buy a bad one, and just reverse all the news I read. It amounts to the same thing. You have the trouble of translating black into white – negative into positive – that is all. Thus, if they say things are bad, I rub my hands with glee; for what is *bad* for them is usually damned *good* for the rest of the world. I am on the side of the *Rest of the World*.'

'What's that?'

'Every decent person must be. There are only two choices possible – to be in on the racket (and lose your soul, if you get me) or *not* be in on it. *Noblesse oblige*. I am compelled to embrace the latter alternative.'

'Oh!' Ossie frowned.

'Therefore their black is my white, and vice versa. It makes newspaper reading quite easy.'

'It sounds nice and simple.'

'It's not quite so simple as that, of course, but that is the principle of the thing, and an uncommonly sound one. I recommend it to you, Osorio!'

'How about the English papers?'

'Just the same.'

'Is that so?'

'The *Manchester Guardian* is the best of them. Always buy it – you can get it anywhere – and just *reverse* everything you read. It is the best "documented" newspaper in England – provided that you turn it all upside down – or read between the lines, *backwards*!'

Ossie gave his fat friend a fresh sidelong glance of great covert hostility and some fear, as they walked along the Paddington platform. 'This man is batty!' he said to himself with conviction. A mad detective! That opened up novel vistas for detective fiction. Detectives (those not professional hacks) were always shrewd supermen, distinguished from less important mortals by the stupendous development of their logical faculties. No, he had never anywhere encountered, that he could remember, a mad detective in mystery books. He had always known of course that old Charlie held odd views upon some topics not like other fellows, to which he had never paid attention. But he had received a very unpleasant funny impression, it was no use denying it, that morning, while in the act of sounding him upon a certain private matter. What was this impression old Charlie had made on him? Well, to state it comprehensively, to all that those two words 'old Charlie' stood for, as they might rise casually in his consciousness, would have to be superadded now something of so unmatey, novel, and suspicious a nature, that 'old Charlie' no longer applied to this fleshly bottle-companion strolling beside him. It was an enigmatical stranger subtly masquerading as 'old Charlie'. So he shot this interloper with all this odd line of talk about matters of so foreign and confusing a nature, another side-long glance, and he perceived, to his dismay, in this placidly-worried exterior a dread something he had never detected there before, which altered its very meaning in the most alarming fashion. He felt, in fact, just as though he suddenly had become aware that one of his most intimate friends was Jack the Ripper – a murderer, yes, *in the flesh*! (And it was of course *the flesh* that he found so disturbing. It is one thing to meet a highly dramatic personage in a book and quite another to have him come rolling up in the light of common day.)

Of course Ossie, so inarticulate to the marrow, did not say this to himself: but, had he detected this disturbing and alien something previous to that, he would certainly have avoided sharing a room with him as he had done the night before, of that we may be tolerably certain.

They had both gone to the Refreshment Saloon and were standing before a couple of large glasses of ale. Both were now silent, Charlie reading the *Journal*, Ossie pondering over the anomalous position involved in being seen off by somebody who had, at the last moment, revealed himself as somebody else. He was in no little perplexity as to how to treat this undesirable associate – whether to say that he was going to his carriage and refuse to recognize the possibility of this well-filled-out, flabbily lantern-jawed, impostor deciding to come round and wish him Godspeed. But something suggested itself to him, as he was pondering dully, a sharp question which filled him of a sudden with intense alarm and caused him to whisk round and carry his hand to his hip-pocket.

Charlie looked up from his paper and said, 'What is it?'

Ossie frowned and he answered with a certain restraint, in referring to such an intimate matter:

'I thought my gat had gone!'

'Oh, is that all?'

'Yes,' said Ossie, and he could not resist the temptation of producing the gat – to the illconcealed uneasiness of a beefy little British burgess at his elbow, who had been quietly watching these two newcomers, and judiciously summing them up, *Journal* and all, as he sipped his Scotch.

The fat young man (no longer quite 'old Charlie') took the weapon in his hand: he frowned down upon it mournfully, like a mastiff examining a King Charles, and then handed it back with a shrug which seemed to go with the French newspaper.

'You couldn't stop a field-mouse with that!' he said.

'Don't you think so?' drawled Oss, flushing to the roots of his hatless head of hair, of Latin black. But he gave the beefy little burgess such a savage look as caused him to start nervously and turn away. Thrusting the snubbed gat back into his hip-pocket, Ossie scowled into the tremendous Refreshment Saloon looking-glass, attempting to catch the eye of the uncomfortable little man of orthodox British beef, redder in the face than ever.

'No,' replied the private inquiry agent superciliously. 'Who on earth sold you that old piece of iron?'

'Oh, I traded it with a fellow who had bought it to commit suicide with for a Brownie I didn't want.'

This odious and corpulent stranger, this erstwhile Charlie, laughed in his face.

'Suicide!' he said. 'What hopes with that baby-boy's peashooter!'

Ossie gave him a very nasty look indeed. He took up his glass of beer and drained it with precision. He cast a ferocious glance at the back of the beefy little burgess, who was hurriedly paying for his Scotch.

'Well ta-ta, Charlie, I must go to my train.'

'I'll come with you – I'd better see you off. You might lose yourself – it's a big station.'

Ossie glared ruggedly: he stopped as they were moving away and said, swallowing hysterically before speaking:

'Don't you have to go to your office?'

'No, I'm not sleuthing today. Come along!'

With this they moved on again. Ossie admitted to himself that he was no match for this madman. Lunatics were not in his line. Ossie got into an empty carriage and sat down while Charlie stood at the door reading the French newspaper. As the guard blew his whistle, Charlie moved to the door, sighed and remarked:

'Well, think over your dark designs, old man.'

'What dark designs are you referring to?'

'Don't carry too much death and destruction among your literary competitors in this party you're going to, with that toy pistol of yours. You might by accident hit one of them in the eye with a pellet and get into hot water. Remember what I said at breakfast about getting jugged. I should throw that stupid thing away.'

Ossie continued to look at him with resentment and misgiving mixed in equal proportions. But, as the train moved off, springing to his feet he thrust his head out of the window and bellowed after the retreating figure of his fat friend the one word:

'MURDERER!'

The percussion of this dreadful vocable upon the hum-drum air – thundered out with the throttle off from a massive pair of lungs, in a tone of over-mastering conviction – caused many a bloodstream to run cold on the instant. Everyone in their neighbourhood upon hearing it looked round in consternation. And their sensations were in no respect modified by observing the evil smile that flitted across the fat young man's unhealthy features.

'That young moron,' the fat young man walking off at a leisurely pace meanwhile was saying to himself, even as he smiled at the commotion that had been caused, 'is as mad as a hatter! No hatter, or hat-wearing person, indeed, could possibly be so mad. He is, I fear, completely demented. What was all that rubbish he was talking about bumping somebody off? Why do they sell children enormous pieces of ordnance like that? – But *They* are mad, as well, that is where it is!'

CHAPTER 4

IGNORANT of the existence of the heavily armed young aspirant to literary renown who was at that moment on his way to join them in a somewhat later train, the Book-World had by now penetrated the Chase: its members had installed themselves in the various rooms assigned to them (according to rank – a big room for a big noise, a little room for a small critical squeak in a minor weekly review), packing the place to the roof in fact, just as a floating Ritz might be packed for a pleasure cruise, a hundred stateroom doors opening and shutting, stewards and stewardesses shepherding the lucky ones about, the lifts congested with luggage, and those with inside berths glaring at those who had secured outside ones. Soon Beverley Chase was full of a portentous crowd enough, to be sure, as to the outward man – shuffling exotics and high-stepping stockbrokers it would seem to any Plain Reader brought there to gaze her fill. It was a mixed crowd of great critics and great authors, leering at the sight of each other as if each and all had been somewhat improper jokes, and moving up and down in animated knots; congratulating each other upon everything (especially upon their books and the splendid reviews of same, and then above all upon the *rich prizes* bestowed upon the said books, and modestly accepted by the prize-winning penman, the 'crowning' of this and of that 'epoch-making' masterpiece – 'Not too strong a word, I stake my critical reputation on it!' – and the masterly puffs that had never ceased to blow the rankest of best-selling hot air – the booming, broadcasting, backing, and boosting, and the sumptuous royalties that went with the above); and all these Good and True Companions of each other, and merry Frothblowers and Puffmakers of each and all, were only restrained from openly scratching each others' backs in the public view by the presence of some frowning and disdainful flunkeys: but all to a man were in each others' pockets and palpably hand-in-glove, and beyond a peradventure visibly saw eye to eye. The radio played softly a sad, sick, jaded Blues, of stalest honeysuckle melody, with a few passionless pansy pats of crushed cymbals – a hottentot fart and a couple of muted slave-driven whines to end up with.

Samuel Shodbutt was constantly, portentously, absent. He was hidden upstairs in a real Book-of-the-Week suite, the Royal Suite, in fact, of Beverley Chase. But there was a great crowd gathered about Lilli O'Stein, the great Austro-Tcheck lady novelist and international log-rolling champion of Middle-Europe. Lilli was more rolled than rolling, but she was universally admitted in England to be the best Good Companion and Jolly Sport of the lot, who would *never* leave a fellow-roller in the lurch or allow his sales to sink below the ten or twelve thousand for want of a good hot puff in any capital in Europe that she was at home in, and she was at home in all.

Now Lilli was a great girl by common consent and so she was rolled up and down, by all the crowd of penmen and pengirls that were there (hot-foot from the latest hot-air rally of the I.N.K. Club), till she was quite red with laughing good-companionate lung-puffs and her mouth ached with being stretched from ear to ear, and it was a good wide one at that. At the other extremity of the hall, near a grove of dwarfed gum-trees and screw-palms, stood the champion puffer of France, who had had loving-cup after loving-cup and gold medals galore. He was Marcel Taxi (you just put up your hand and called out *taxi!* and if you had the right sort of face he would take you – on a special tariff – to whatever I.N.K. Club or other similar institution your business required you to visit). He had a lank, sad bitter jowl and a fish's eye but there was no fairer man in the book-world. Hemmed in by a fawning francophile throng, he made the rafters ring with his parleyvous until his court was broken up by the unexpected appearance of a coal-black mammie, who fell upon his neck and burst into a tropical storm of Southern sobs. At once the impression was created that some relationship, avowed or otherwise, existed between these two, ill-assorted as they might at first sight appear. This false impression was afterwards dispelled. There was of course no relationship. Mrs Wellesley-Crook had been a Crook of Chicago, with a verandahed château in the South, in the Old Dominion, where she was connected with the aristocratic Blackwood Toyts, and this was her old mammie, more or less. That was all. This honest period-Black, fit for a stage-plantation, had heard it said that Mounseer Taxi had written a swell life of Booker or of George Washington – a beautiful thing full of golden tears and she just had to thank him *personally* to his face, it was her simple black way. But behold, the moment she had clapped eyes upon that sweet kind face of his (which looked so full of understanding of any dark downtrodden, faithful, thick-lipped stock like hers – from way-down below such a line as the Mason–Dixon Line), her heart just swept her right off her feet. Before she could say Jack Robinson (or Booker Washington) she had found herself all a-sob upon his broad Jura-bred chest, which sported the scarlet pip of the *Legion* (honour to whom honour is due!) as some trifling recompense for his services to Anglo-American Letters and indirectly to French Letters – from Corneille to Cocteau and after, but especially to the transatlantic field – he knew Hollywood like his pocket and was far more at home on Bunker Hill than on the Butte Chaumont.

Several of the older of the onlookers were moved, too, very much, as was only to be expected. They turned aside – they *se mouchaient*, as Shodbutt would have said.

'I do think Marcel Taxi is so *original*!' one of these non-celebrated people, with a walking-on part, exclaimed, as moist-eyed he watched the great international penman pat the humble plantation mammie's woolly head – a scene that if he had not received an invitation to this historic gathering he would certainly not have been privileged to witness.

'Yes, where there are so many imitators and even plagiarists these days . . . !'

'I know.'

'The French are not usually original.'

'No, *we* are more . . .'

'Taxi is an exception.'

'He got a prize, did he not, for originality?'

'Yes – for the most original book-review of the year. The Year's Most Original Book-Review. It is a French prize.'

'Yes, I remember.'

'He did not *once* make use of the word "genius". And yet, in spite of that, he conveyed that a greater writer had never lived. Let me see, who was it he was doing?'

'Yes, I was trying to remember!'

'Oh, of course! It was Lilli O'Stein!'

'Of course it was! She's a great girl, is Lilli!'

'She is indeed. It is strange how the *Irish* comes out in her prose.'

'In the German?'

'No, I meant in the translation. But no doubt in German it is also . . .'

'Of course. But is she then Irish?'

'The O, you know.'

'Oh!'

'O'Stein.'

'Ah yes, of course. She is the greatest writer in Germany . . .'

'Or Ireland for that matter!'

'Yes, I suppose Ireland could claim . . .'

'She is very proud of her descent.'

'Which? The Irish? How is it that the O . . . ?'

'Oh, *that* is all that is left.'

'Just the O . . . ?'

'And the apostrophe.'

A certain embarrassment overtakes both of the two Fleet Street onlookers and hangers-on at this point and they hurriedly change the subject, as if they had been inadvertently drawn into a topic relating to lavatories 'before ladies'. A little guiltily they turn tail, even, and, as they converse, now in undertones, pass into a less crowded part of the hall, their four pale spats moving up and down in time.

Marcel kisses the curly head of the coal-black mammie, amid applause and a tender accompaniment of good-companionate laughter. Curtsying to the earth the honest negress retires backwards. Taxi kisses his hand. More applause.

CHAPTER 5

LADY SALTPETER is the sister of Mrs Wellesley-Crook and the mother of the Hon. Baby Bucktrout. She and her daughter now met and they were talking over what Miss Corse did when Baby Bucktrout was fresh with Tom. They were in their rooms in the North Tower. The Tool House was under the windows. The gardeners were in the Tool House. Their drawls came up from beneath and there were the distinct sounds of rough horticultural guffaws. A vein of boisterous lubricity ran through the joking tones of the talkative gardeners. Tom their butt was there in the Tool House with them.

'This place would not be so terribly bad if it were not for old Corse,' Baby was saying, all dollish pugnacity, and spoiling for a stand-up altercation with Corse (but with menial handicap for once *in full force*, and the feudal immunity of the master — with *carte blanche* this time for the Baby to manhandle the *Bonne*).

'I daresay,' said her mother.

'Corse is out of hand.'

'Is she?'

'Very much so. She's above herself altogether. It's time Corse was put firmly in her place. I am black and blue — the old wretch!'

'Are you?'

'Yes, I am. How would *you* like to be snatched up and carried indoors like a child, just when you were on the point of enjoying yourself?'

'I should not relish that, I have never said I should.'

'No! Life is *not* all honey, is it?'

'Hardly.'

'No. One can't afford to lose any *drips* that come one's way — that's all it amounts to.' Baby scratched her flank with a varnished fingernail where there was an itchy bruise from her last encounter with Corse.

'I thought you did not exactly wait for it to come your way. That, if I am not mistaken, is the trouble.'

'And if one just *stayed put*, mother — what then? You are so unbearably brutal — you and your bashibazouks. There is *not* enough to go round these days — ask anybody! — in the way of what your lot called men-folk. Man-flesh is at a premium — in our walk of life.'

'Dear me — you talk as if we lived in a butcher's shop.'

'Yes, I know! But there was a great plenty in your young days — you lived in a period flowing with milk and honey. Men used to go about with their tongues hanging out when you were my age.'

'I've heard your views on that subject before. You are spoilt, that's what it is. My fault, I know, but still!'

'I like that! You know there is no milk, much less honey, anywhere for *us* — unless we go and dig for it! That is what I was doing as a matter of fact.'

'Yes. I quite understand that. Corse told me what you were doing.'

'Yes. And that old *busybody* burst in and — oh! I could murder her! Would she dare to interfere with *a bee* — as it was about to suck its — *pollen*? Is it pollen?'

'I daresay. But you are not a bee, are you? I am surprised at your comparing yourself with such an animal.'

'No, that is the trouble — I am *not*. I understand that all right. It is because I'm *human* that I am treated in this revolting way! No bee would stand it for a minute.'

'I don't understand you.'

'If I were *a bee* no one – but *no one*! – would dare to treat me – would dream of treating me!'

'No – if you were an insect, perhaps not.'

'No. *There would be my sting!*'

'Yes, I can see that. I can imagine that as a matter of fact.'

'Oh what an oversight! Why have I not a gwate big *sting?*'

Baby Bucktrout made a gesture indicating the dimensions of the sting required by any really well-equipped human being at the present time: and it appeared to be a formidable weapon.

Lady Saltpeter dreamily closed her eyes – the dramatic flight of the Queen Bee flashed across her mind, as reported by Maeterlinck, and next she was off to Covent Garden, beside the stage-lagoon with Pelléas and Mélisande. Recalled to a sense of duty, she opened her eyes again, mildly alert.

'What did you say you would do, mother, if somebody seized you at the moment when you were enjoying yourself? I forget what you said.'

'I said nothing.'

'I thought not.'

'But that is not the point, my dear Baby.' Her ladyship was very calm and aloofly horsey, she smoked a big cigarette – big for a cigarette but small for a cigar.

'I beg your pardon,' said Baby. 'If the point does not lie there I fail to see where it does, Lady Saltpeter.'

Lady Saltpeter whinnied like a very wave-lined inbred mount indeed, unexpectedly indisposed. It was a sigh – she regarded her daughter across the gulf that was between them – an impassable gulf.

'Your ideas of pleasure are so peculiar, Baby. That is what is the matter.'

'How about your own, mother?'

Lady Saltpeter sniffed and squared her shoulders, and thrust out her huge mountebank-chin, of far-fetched animality.

'Corse shows her good sense, I think,' she said, 'by the action she took. She is really quite right to remove you if she finds you in the Tool House. You should not go into the Tool House. It is ridiculous always to be found in the Tool House.'

'There are more ridiculous places than a Tool House.'

'Is there nowhere else you can go? Besides, you are not wanted there it seems. It is absurd; you must see that.'

Baby laughed harshly. There was a hoarse rumble of laughter, too, from the Tool House, which entered at the open window. Lady Saltpeter looked up and raised her eyebrows and stuck out her jaw. The roughishness of the gang of gardeners brought to the surface a few dilapidated aristocratic instincts.

'Well,' said her mother then. 'We have to discuss this. We must discuss it, whether we like it or not.'

'I suppose so.'

'Can you give me any good reason why you should prefer dirty agricultural robots, who work in hedges and ditches, to gentlemen? After all it *is* absurd, you must see that.'

'Is it?' asked Baby. And she laughed hoarsely like a laughing-doll, in short mechanical gasps.

'Well, I should like very much to hear, Baby, what you have to say to that all the same, if you will oblige me by providing *some* answer while we are on the subject.'

'Very good, I can't have an affair with *a Quean*, now, can I, mother darling. *It Takes Two to Make a Bedroom-Scene!*'

'If we agree to that, nevertheless, all young men are not what you call them. What are queens, however – effeminate, I suppose?'

'The opposite to kings. When you live under a monarchi-
cal system . . .'

'Quite, quite! We appear to be talking at cross-purposes.'

'Somewhat. There are queans and queens – of course I
meant the former – the American variety.'

'An *American* queen! It was a great mistake to send you to
America. It has muddled you somewhat. However. You
mentioned *It Takes Two to Make a Bedroom-Scene!* I should
have thought now that the author of that . . .'

'What, Donald?'

'Butter – something.'

'Oh, Donald is a *roaring* quean. He is the world's quean.'

'What on earth is a *roaring queen*? It is an objectionable
expression, I consider – it sounds to me like *Alice in Wonder-
land*, where there are a number of peculiar queens, if I remember rightly, only it is vulgar, like everything American.'

'I will try not to be vulgar, Lady Saltpeter. Donald and I
were engaged last month but Donald is not a marrying man
you understand.'

'Why the engagement then?'

'He is defective in those strong sexual instincts that alone
make the married state the success it should be. It is not his
fault, but there it is: make what you can of it.'

'How do you know? Besides that may be a passing . . .'
her ladyship hesitated and then with a squeamish upper lip
she picked the word 'phase'.

'Phase!'

Lady Saltpeter sniffed delicately.

'I'm afraid not, such things do not *pass* so easily,' Baby
replied.

'No?'

'Not Donald. He was born that way. He is, whatever the
reason, especially unsuited to go to the altar. He is no son-
in-law for you, believe me.'

Lady Saltpeter shrugged her wide, strapped-down, smart-tailored shoulders – which had been to the altar, however paradoxically, and where one pair of shoulders can go, there *another* pair of shoulders can go: or so her shoulders said.

'I have not considered these questions for a long time. Some boys are more precocious than others, certainly. Are there not *transformations*, too – as in the world of insects? Rather uncanny.'

'No they don't change. Donald's a washout, believe me – I've tested him inside-out, he's every inch a dud.'

'I like, what do you call him, Donald Butterboy. He is a most brilliant young man – perhaps like all geniuses he is ...'

'Geniuses! Oh *boy*! Genius! Donald! No!'

'Next week he will probably receive, so I am told, the Book of the Week Prize,' Lady Saltpeter replied with the air of impassably producing a splendid trump.

'That may be. But he laughs at *that* even himself! The Book of the Week Prize! That is a standing joke with every undergraduate. Didn't you know? They all get that sooner or later – at least those who scribble their lives and make it into a novel – *all*! I could get it next week if I wanted it.'

'No, I did not know that.'

'Every fool gets *that*.'

'I did not know of course. But he is supposed, so Maisie says, to have a very good chance with this novel he has written, what is it called, yes, *It Takes Two to Make a Bedroom-Scene!* – of getting the Sévigné-Stavisky Award as well, founded by a great Parisian financier ...'

'I know – Stavisky – simply lousy with money: but a great guy they say. Veronica Schwartzschild knows him quite well.'

'And Maisie says that probably he will also be awarded the Novel League of Greater Britain, also a prize given by the Genius of the Semester Club – have I got that right? – both these as well will be won by this novel of his.'

'*And* the Hawthorn Bush, or whatever it is, and a few more! But there is one prize old Donald'll never be getting, and that's a prize as a high-pushing He-man, you get me! He would make the world's worst bridegroom would D. Butterboy. You may take my word for that. And *I'm* not going to be the bride!'

'You insist upon employing a terminology a little unfamiliar to me.'

'Of course you are not familiar with it. How should you be – it is used with reference to practices, mother dear, which have never appealed to you.'

'I am glad to say they have not.'

'But let us talk about what you understand!'

'Really, Baby. It does not matter to me what you do – it is not a pleasure to be your mother.'

'I know. How did you manage it, anyway?'

'I am doing *my best* – for *both of us*. This is not a motiveless or unselfish conversation, I hope you understand.'

'The performance is a poor one. Perhaps because we are discussing the duller types of love.'

'I certainly agree that what we are discussing is *dull*.'

'Now if it were Diana Doughty with whom you were conversing!'

Lady Saltpeter rose abruptly and her left eye flashed – the other remained unmoved.

'I cannot listen to this – Diana is a great friend of mine, it is unnecessary to drag her in. It is not part of the bargain.'

'What bargain?'

'I don't see why I should have my friends dragged in. Even a functional creature, like a mother . . . !'

'Do sit down, mother. Since Corse man-handled me the sight of any determined female, upon her feet and looking as if she meant business, gives me the jitters. You really have succeeded in sending me into a cold sweat — look!'

Lady Saltpeter sat down again.

'Very well,' she said. 'But I wish I could make you understand, Baby . . .'

'All right. But it is your fault if I am like I am.'

'Indeed. That is something new to me.'

'Not so new as all that. It is all your Edwardianism, you know, that is to blame at bottom.'

'My what?'

'It is all the horrible unnatural wickedness of you Edwardians that has produced *me*.'

'Really!'

'It is all the beastly unnatural vices of *your period*, Lady Saltpeter, that is responsible for me, such as I am. You should consider yourself lucky it's not worse than it is. I *might* have been *anything*! Absolutely anything.'

'To what period, please, are you referring, Baby?'

'I even blush to name it!'

'That is a promising sign.'

'But still one is compelled sometimes to speak out. I referred of course to the,' Baby lowered her voice, 'the — the *Nineties*.'

'Oh. Those. Is that all?'

'After such an epoch one had to *do something* to clear the air.'

'You call it clearing the air!'

'At least that's how I feel about it. With a mother who belongs to what was probably one of the most decadent periods in English history . . .'

'Really, Baby. I think you must have been dipping into some book.'

'Am I not speaking the truth, mother? The *worst* of us today are pale imitations of what your lot were in the — I won't say it again! I don't like saying it! In the *you-know-whats*!'

'Yes, I know which you mean – you have told me. In the Nine . . .'

Baby (frantically): 'Yes – *them*!'

'I must say I think you are hard on . . .'

'Hard on! Think what it means to *us*. As a small child look what I had to fight against. I at least am *natural*. But *you* . . .'

Lady Saltpeter rose majestically and quickly.

'Baby!'

'I shall simply leave you, mother, if you insist upon standing up!'

Lady Saltpeter resumed her seat.

'Very well, Baby – I prefer sitting down, as a matter of fact. I am not so young as I was in the Nine . . .'

Baby stamped her foot and shouted, 'You shameless old woman! I won't have Them mentioned in my presence!'

'You referred to them *first*!'

'You and yours,' and Baby pointed the finger of theatrical denunciation at Lady Saltpeter, 'you have ruined all of *us* – all you Edwardian devils incarnate in that Sodom and Gomorrah of a time of yours – it is *you* who made us what we are, and then you have the *toupet* to come and preach to us! It is absolutely revolting! Yes, I'm going to give you a piece of my mind this time, Lady Saltpeter, it's no use your thinking you can escape. Take *me* – what has happened to me?'

'What, indeed? I have often asked myself that question.'

'I shudder when I think of the risks I have run. I am *ashamed* at the shifts to which I have been put to go straight. I am compelled to read *Lady Chatterley's Lover*, if you please, and such books as that, in order to prevent myself from falling back into the vices upon which I was nurtured – which in the cradle were insinuated into my suckling-milk – yes, that with my first lisp I was taught to prattle of!'

'But what is this! I am not responsible for what happened in the . . . Allow me to point out . . . !'

'No. It is only by the skin of my teeth that I have escaped! And then to crown everything you have the sublime effrontery to send, or Aunt Maisie does, her horrid *Cossacks* – such an old ruffian as Corse – to *ill-treat* me, when I am doing all I can to save myself from being like – like – like the likes of *you*! Ugh!'

'I like that! Me! I am not *a period* after all!'

Baby Bucktrout with a great sob of indignation flung herself down at full length upon a settee and buried her face in her hands. There she wept convulsively for a few moments – and the sound of ignorant indelicate horseplay came in through the open window from the Tool House beneath.

Lady Saltpeter lit a cigarette and shut up, with a hard-boiled click, her cigarette case.

'Your emotional outlook on life plays you strange tricks,' said Lady Saltpeter.

'Booo-ooooo-oooo!' said Baby.

'I am not saying that we in the Nine . . .'

With the leap of a wild-cat, Baby Bucktrout was upon her feet, eyes streaming with tears but flashing through the cascades, with hands horribly clenched.

'Mother, I *forbid* you to *mention* them in any way whatever, you understand! I *will* not sit here – I will not lie here – and have you sit there, and in the most matter-of-fact way possible *talk* about them as if they were nothing more than – oh than any other Time, when you know that they are responsible for your daughter and all that you – you' (with great pathos) 'reproach her with!'

'But, darling, please remember that the Nine . . .'

'Mother!' screamed Baby Bucktrout, beside herself. 'I *will* not tolerate it! You have not a shred of respect for me left!'

'I could scarcely be aware,' said Lady Saltpeter, 'how strongly you felt upon that subject. But I still have to discuss with you a tiresome matter of some practical importance. *To both of us.*'

Baby, seated upon the settee, wiping her eyes with the backs of her hands, observed her ladyship as a cat a mouse, in wait for the appearance of that deadly numeral.

'Whether Donald – er Butter something – is as you say he is . . .'

'What can you still have to discuss with me about Donald Butterboy?'

Baby focused her parent with a fishy eye of glum restraint.

'Well, the Book of the Week Prize . . .'

'Well – the Book of the Week Prize – what then?'

'This young man has shown himself capable of being attracted by you – Maisie is my informant. Calf love perhaps. But Butterboy knows which side his bread is buttered too. Next Monday morning he will wake up, it is predicted, and find himself famous – like Byron.'

'Will he?' sneered Baby. 'Well, what of it?'

'He will then of course be a famous author. You may choose to sniff at that . . .'

'He won't be the *first* famous author of that sort nor the last.'

'I suppose you mean by that, Baby, that it occurs every week?'

'I do. Sometimes there are four of them in a week – they share it like a lottery ticket.'

'However . . .'

'You should only hear Raymond Pawnsfoot, mother, on the subject of the Book of the Week Prize!'

'Raymond Pawnsfoot is a nice boy, but he is embittered.'

'What about?'

'Well, he got it a year ago, and he has of course been eclipsed fifty times at least since then, I suppose, as there are fifty weeks in the year. It *does* make anyone bitter, I expect: so *many* times! Evidently he is unpleasant about this prize. You would be stupid to pay too much attention to that.'

'Anyhow, it *must* be a pretty dud prize if old Donald is going to get it!'

'No man is a prophet in his own nursery.'

'True. But a Quean with a swelled head is a thousand times worse than one who has never woken up on a Monday and found himself famous till Saturday.'

'That remains to be seen,' said Lady Saltpeter. 'But never mind about that; at the present moment you simply must consent to consider the future a little, for your sake, and of course for mine. I have a future, too, though you are probably unaware of the fact.'

'How can *I* think about the future – much less you! – with a *Past*...!'

Baby Bucktrout showed signs of emotional disintegration as she referred to the Past – that Past in which the Naughty N's bulked so lurid and so large.

'There will be plenty of time later on for what you were doing in the Tool House. You will even, perhaps, have a Tool House of your own. Far more convenient, you know.'

'There's no time like the present!' squeaked Baby Bucktrout.

Lady Saltpeter shrugged her shoulders.

'That is stupid.'

'I think not.' Baby scratched her tumefied flanklet.

'I regard it as stupid.'

'But I tell you I hate effeminate boys who write books or do Gossip. It is only with workmen or with servants that you are sure of finding *the Goods*, and I don't mind saying so!'

'Find the *what*, darling?'

'I want the Goods – you understand? I must have *the Goods*!'

Lady Saltpeter sniffed.

'You have more vitality than ever I had, my dear – I'm not sure, however, if that is a matter for congratulation.'

'But I'm not *you*, see? Can't you grasp that fact?'

'Very well. We agree to differ.'

'Absolutely.'

'What next? For we do not seem to make much progress.'

'What have all these beastly people been brought down for today?' asked Baby, listening to the sweet music of gruff voices coming up from the Tool House.

'How should I know? I did not ask them to come here.'

'About Donald's book? But it's tripe – you said so yourself.'

'I said nothing of the sort.'

'Yes you did – yesterday,' barked Baby.

'No. I don't remember ever having expressed . . . I don't see that that matters either – I was not talking about *my* opinion of these aspirants to fame.'

'Perhaps not. Well, you're not going to get me off on one of Butterboy's kidney, so you needn't run away with that idea. And if you send Corse after me again, I will *stab* her.'

'Darling!'

'With this!'

Baby laughed hoarsely. She produced a stiletto. Her mother was a determined-looking woman even for her character and size: she stepped over resolutely to the window and gazed out of it at the Tool House.

'It would be idle for me to pretend,' Lady Saltpeter said

after a few moments of intense contemplation of the Tool House, 'that I object at all to your killing Miss Corse with a stiletto. I do not.'

Baby laughed harshly and very recklessly.

'It is not that at all,' her ladyship continued. 'To put the matter bluntly, I do not wish to have you on my hands any longer than I can help.'

'I have been on Aunt Maisie's hands mostly.'

'I regret for selfish motives that you should do things calculated to interfere with your "getting off", as you refer to it.'

'I see. You don't give a hoot whether I lie with the assistant gardeners . . .'

'Of course not.'

'But you wish me to wed a half-man, and so be rid of me?'

'You have often ventured to criticize my conduct. Excuse me if I too am outspoken.'

'Very well. If Miss Corse interferes with me again!'

'If only you make a good job of it, darling, you will no doubt be hanged, and that will be an end of the matter — every bit as satisfactory, as far as I am concerned, as if you are married. Perhaps more so.'

Baby laughed more hoarsely yet. She hid her stiletto.

'Ah, you Edwardians! What a period! What a *cesspool*! Oh!'

'But do not let us quarrel, Baby, over this,' said Lady Saltpeter, returning from the window. 'You were brought up here — and in America. It is natural Miss Corse should mother you — a little roughly, it is her way. Why not let her do so? She possesses the maternal instinct, much more strongly than I do, I am quite sure. Why not be guided by her?'

'Be bullied by Old Corse? Never!'

'But she is certainly in the right with regard to the gardeners and other menservants.'

Baby laughed boisterously and bitterly.

'I'm not going to be fobbed off with scribbling fairies – I must have the Goods, and that's flat! I will have the Goods!' she exclaimed in fierce incantation. 'A Man or nothing. No half-man for me!'

'Certainly, certainly, and so you shall. But you can't go out into the garden with a lassoo to catch the gardeners, darling, without attracting unfavourable comment, my pet.'

'What do I care for the comment – any more than in your time, you have, have you?'

'You even *enjoy* the comment, of course. You are such a little self-advertiser. You are almost a mountebank, I am rather afraid.'

Baby laughed in a hollow way and turned her back upon her mother.

'But you must forfeit *some* of the things you enjoy, else you forfeit *all*, of course. That is the rule of life, if I am not mistaken. Why not give up *advertisement?*'

'Why don't you?'

'I? I haven't appeared in a gossip par for ten years and more, quite that.'

'What a lie! I saw you mentioned only last week!'

'I am sure you are confusing me with someone else.'

Lady Saltpeter stood up and examined herself in the glass. She turned to Baby and looked her up and down with a disgusted eye.

'Well, that is that,' she said. 'Let us go down and see the Lions. I believe I caught sight of Mr Samuel Shodbutt a moment ago upon the terrace, when I was looking out of the window. He has something of Doctor Johnson in him, I always feel. It is surprising how the eighteenth century seems to go on cropping up in our characters, don't you agree? That is much more my period, too, than the Nineties . . .'

A book violently hurtled, like a goose in flight, past Lady Saltpeter's head, and she passed out of the door.

CHAPTER 6

FROM the windows of the Royal Suite Samuel Shodbutt and Joanie Shodbutt surveyed the garden: Shodbutt was thrust forward with frowning pugnacity, showing himself more than Mrs S.S. Someone pointed up at the principal window of the Royal Suite, crying evidently, 'Oh! there is Shodbutt lodged, *of course*, in the most important rooms in the castle.' And Shodbutt observed the pointing finger, and he showed himself in the window with a more threatening manner than even before. Yes, Shodbutt was there! Look your fill, young man! Shodbutt is *all there*!

Guests had strolled out in little parties. They were looking about them, they were taking stock of the magnificence of the setting in which Big Business spelt by Books had enabled them to find themselves – in happy conjunction it is understood with the Chicagoan wealth of the Crooks, and the evil times upon which the Wellesleys had fallen – that was a necessary component of this scintillating situation, too. Mr Wellesley-Crook, their host, pointed at a tree, and then at another tree. The tree pranced about in the wind as if to show off its plumage to the guests.

But the angry eyes of Shodbutt were directed elsewhere. In scornful long-range indolence they focused upon five figures. These loitered upon the brink of the basin of a small piece of water. Three of them were the committee of the Sévigné-Stavisky Award – for The Year's Best Autobiography. Never once had the mighty Shodbutt been invited to form one of this exclusive literary tribunal. That was a great outrage. And consequently he lay in wait for the books of the Sévigné-Stavisky Award in the pages of the *Morning Outcry* with a sullen gaze; and he greeted their appearance with more than a blustering sniff of the pen.

Two of this group were Cambridge-bred highbrows — sickly *light-blues* with pale blue eyes (attracted by the fat prize from France, and laying their traps for an early award for a little autobiographical *opus* which one of the two was revolving in her brain, timing it for the next Sévigné-Stavisky prize-giving). Furthermore, one of the members of the committee was French: and, for these pallidly excitable provincials, to hail from France was tremendous: *Oui, Oui!* carried it every time over *Yes, Yes!*

And if the gaze of Samuel Shodbutt fell more ponderously in one place than another, it oppressed, if anything, more peculiarly that drooping intellect-ravaged exterior of the lanky and sickly lady in Victorian muslins — the greater and more world-famous of the pair of mind-proud, vacantly staring — for no banns ever published would devirginate either of those colossal spinsters. Yes! there, beneath his very eyes, wilted pretentiously the very woman who had but a few months ago written a vile supercilious pamphlet all about Shodbutt. And it had been a very insulting piece of work indeed. So the highly finished Victorian languor of the patronizing queen of the highbrow world (whose pen had but yesterday allowed itself to be facetious at the expense of the scribbling grocer puffed up into a Brummagem critical Lion) attracted the darkest sparks from his smouldering eye-socket — and Shodbutt's chin was puckered like a disgruntled patch of ocean ruffled into a snarling surface by a storm — and the drooping extremities of his moustache whiskered dankly the contemptuous corners of his mouth. The haughty Shodbutt eyed the little distant drooping image of best faded Victorian *chic* and he considered what remark, if any, he should make when they came face to face downstairs.

'There's Rhoda Hyman,' was all he said to his attendant wife.

'So I see,' said Joanie darkly. 'I noticed her at once. She will get the Sévigné-Stavisky next autumn or my name's not Shodbutt – I feel it in my bones.'

Shodbutt grunted at Sévigné-Stavisky. He hoped that Mrs Hyman would, and *he* would have something to say about it – about the prize and about her – in his weekly article, and what he said would enlighten her a little bit as to where she got off – in posterity if not in the bogus present of the amateur's heyday.

Just then a tall and over-willowly young apparition emerged: running first with a halting grace (evidently frustrated by the roguishness of a wilful lock of hair of vivid whisky-green, which he dashed away first from one eye then the other, to see where he was going more clearly), he swayed out in slow-time into the centre of an immaculate green lawn, with a most marked queenly squeamishness of bashful deportment. At once the face of S.S. cleared up as if by magic. He looked hard at the attractive figure upon the lawn, he looked again, then broadly grinned right down upon it.

Yes – Shodbutt was not deceived – this must be he! That human gazelle was *his*, His protégé!

'Joanie – that must be young Donald Butterboy!' the great man grated with grim satisfaction. Next Monday, or rather Tuesday or the Tuesday after that, young Butterboy would wake up and find himself famous. And it would be the great Shodbutt who would ring the bells and blow the trumpets – indeed was it not really Shodbutt who was *Fame*? Shodbutt was Destiny! Shodbutt was Time's Whirligig! Shodbutt was its heart!

'Where?' asked Mrs S.S. in affected eager surprise. 'Oh yes, I see him! Yes, I recognize him from the photograph. It *is* Donald Butterboy — you are right, S.S.!'

'It's him all right! — A marvellous piece of writing for a boy of twenty, that last chapter in *It Takes Two to Make a Bedroom-Scene!*' growled the omnipotent critic, eyeing possessively *his* next week's 'genius', and fiercely scrutinizing the rival group once more. *They* had no Butterboys up their sleeve, that he would wager! And even if they *had*, still they unquestionably could not boast a trumpet that carried as far as did his, to the four corners of the world of letters. Could not he, Shodbutt, with a single blast, transform *any* Butterboy whatever for that matter into a more famous 'genius' than they could ever concoct, with *all* their international puffs? Between ourselves, was it not Shodbutt's *trumpet* (not the brains of a Butterboy) that was *it*? — the 'genius' was really the critic's. This *entre nous — n'est-ce pas?* The magic lay in the *puff*. And he, Shodbutt, had the *ne plus ultra* peach of a megaphone: and if all the lot blew wildly together they could not blow such a bubble as *he* could blow — to marry two beautiful metaphors, the Cherubim and Pears' Soap.

'And the first chapter,' said Joanie. 'That is even better.'

'I haven't read the first chapter. I never read the first chapters!'

'Oh darling, I know, but *that* first . . . !'

'I can well believe it — I bet it was. Deep, eh? You needn't tell me — I only had to read the last page. I took my hat off at once. I knew it was *genius*.'

'It is. It is,' she turned up her eyes, which squinted slightly, 'geeen-ius!'

'It was the last line that decided me. It carried me off my feet.'

'Mine too!'

'The last line. On the last page. I said *This is the goods*. And I'm not often wrong. I could tell it at a glance.'

'There was one in the middle . . .'

'I remember that – I remember – you told me about it. A chapter full of genius, wasn't it? It must have been.'

'No, it was a line.'

'I remember it! It went deep – *a line only*. Marvellous. I never read the middle of a book. A quoi bon!'

'En effet!'

'Cela ne rîme à rien.'

'Tu as raison, cher S.S.'

'The middle of anything is *always* a bore. Even with such a book as *It Takes Two to Make a Bedroom-Scene!*, it is a bore. The middle cannot be anything but a bore.'

'How I agree with you! There are very few books that bear reading in the middle. For me *c'est le premier pas qui coûte*.'

'Not for me – not for me! It all lies in *the last page*.'

'Of course, the last page . . .'

'I *never* read more than the last page. Balzac said he knew what a book was like without even opening it. I can't say that – that's more than I can claim – I take off my hat to Balzac! He was a *genius*! No. I have to *open* them. It's no use – I admit it, I have to open them. But I never need to go farther than the last page.'

'I know!'

'If that doesn't stir me, I just shut it up with a bang, and mark it N.G. But give me a last page – and I'm infallible. Infallible.'

'You would be infallible even if you never opened . . .'

'No, no. Balzac – *Balzac*! Not me! I take off my hat to Balzac! I must *open* it!

'You do yourself an injustice.'

'No. I can't tell if a book has genius unless I open it. No, Joanie – not without opening it!'

'But Sam, darling, often you *haven't*. It has been sufficient for me to *tell* you, in a nutshell . . .'

'That is true. Nutshell. Yes!'

'It is perfectly marvellous the way *the slightest hint* – why one word sometimes is enough. I have known you to decide upon the title alone!'

'That is true, yes. There have been times. I have often done that. A title – I *have* done it with only the title. But that's risky, Joanie! Risky!'

'I think your *flair* is unbelievable! I am positive that if I told Balzac the little that I have sometimes told *you*, he would never have been able to judge unerringly – to judge as you have always done. Not even Flaubert could!'

'Ah, *Flaubert*! I take off my hat to Flaubert! Flaubert was a genius! He would have told at once – even if the book had never been written.'

'I believe he could! But so could you – you know you could, S.S.!'

But S.S.'s brow became like thunder. He swelled out his person suddenly as if his stomach would explode with a sudden influx of ungovernable wrath.

'What's that young fool doing?' he breathed fiercely forth – at his fullest distention, of a dangerous newspaper celebrity, who at a word can damn and shrivel up.

'What is it, Samuel?' alarmed, asked his better-half.

'Do you see where Butterboy has gone?' he asked. 'Do you see where the young fool has gone?'

Mrs S.S. approached the window, and in a moment her face sympathetically reported that she *had* seen and registered a heavy drop in temperature.

'Yes. I see, indeed,' she said.

'The young fool!'

'Fool indeed,' she echoed.

'I'll bet he's after the Sévigné-Stavisky.'

'I shouldn't be surprised, even at that.'

And the two stood gazing down at the distinguished clusters of animated and unanimated figures, whose hobby or whose trade was lettered fame. And yes, there were now *six* figures instead of five figures upon the brink of the small ornamental sheet of water. *And the sixth was that of Donald Butterboy.* There were no two ways about that.

CHAPTER 7

RHODA HYMAN saw that the newcomer was after the prize from the way he came up and she gave Donald Butterboy a stand-off reception for her part. She could tell, she thought, from the waggle of his flanks that he thought the prize was as good as his already. But the big man on the committee (a great Caledonian Proust-fan who was a great follower of the frousty proustian Eros, and inclined to young Butterboy from the first moment Donald had stepped out upon the grass) took him at once by the arm and asked him pointblank about his novel. The susceptible Scot could see at once that it probably had 'genius'. Twice now he had passed over the great Rhoda (two seasons running) for the male sex and for the same reason – namely through finding them *per se* as a sex more interesting, and who's to blame him? Mrs Hyman knew this and she dreaded him particularly, for she knew she might never get it, being of The Sex. But the French member of the committee, *he* would cast his vote upon the feminist side – for he had designs upon the Literary Province of London and unquestionably Rhoda possessed a powerful following there. All this had been put into his, well you know, coldly-logical head by much desultory observation amongst these comic islanders – with difficulty it had dawned on him that the children of the Third Republic went down *very well indeed* with the Liberal British, especially those of a radical literary turn, stemming from old Victorian stocks of monied 'rebels' in poke-bonnets and crinolines, established in suburban castles, in imitation of Strawberry Hill: and from noticing (he was not very intelligent but he couldn't help it) how they mistook all French-speaking riff-raff (of which he was a pretty raffish exemplar) for blood-brothers of Talleyrand and de La Rochefoucauld, the poor snobbish boobs of sentimental Brits! So, though his name was only Jacques Jolat and he had left it at that, and he customarily confined himself to employing his pen as a puffing machine, for daily hire, he had a little book in mind as well. So he *oui-oui-cher-maîtred* a goodish bit with the Empress of highbrow London and she on her side was positive she had his vote for the little thing she had in her head too – that is provided Butterboy did not win by foul means. But she could see he was a fearful flirt and it would be a close thing. Meanwhile she felt positively back in the French *ancien régime* with all these *parfaitements* and *je pense biens* dashing about her ears – in fancy amongst a golden company, upon the polished lawns of the Sun King; though she could not help remarking and could not understand it that Monsieur Jolat, deliciously bearded as he was, had (for a Frenchman) almost a *common* look. And her mind stole dreamily away – she thought of dear Monsieur Taxi (who was so important that he had left hurriedly almost at once after lunch, he had so many engagements he had only been able to come for an hour or two), he was certainly a more perfect specimen of his race than this corpulent Monsieur Jolat. But Taxi would influence his countryman she felt sure. No, Mrs Rhoda Hyman would certainly put up a good fight for the Sévigné-Stavisky, which she coveted more than all the British prizes put together, for to be crowned in the Literary Province of London, or Oxford or Cambridge, was one thing, but the capital of Europe, Paris, was quite another, and it would bring her into contact with numbers of Frenchmen, like Monsieur Jolat here, and Frenchwomen, like La Princesse de Périgorde, the immensely

wealthy Communist and drug addict. So in a sickly, tired –
intense and lackadaisical – fashion the dreamy old Rhoda
yearned deeply and drearily for the Sévigné-Stavisky Award
for a Work of Authentic Autobiography – 'For the encour-
agement of a fearless Exhibitionism – Open to Men as well.
Under special circumstances'. There seemed nothing *but*
special circumstances, bitterly reflected Rhoda, her eyes
passing in a wild melancholy swoop over Butterboy.

Mrs Rhoda Hyman was so absorbed in all this that
Samuel Shodbutt was able to approach unnoticed, and bluffly
he broke into the delicious turning-movements of her discreet campaign – all carried on in what was once the tongue
of Madame de Sévigné and was now the tongue of Stavisky,
hence the marriage of these two not dissimilar names.

'Well, well,' the great book-critic of the *Morning Outcry*
gruffly stuttered in her ear: 'Mrs Hyman has, I see, forsaken
the Tavistock quarter of Town! *Quel chance!* I did not guess,
when I said I would come down here, that I should see *you*
of all people.'

'Nor I that I should see you,' Mrs Rhoda retorted faintly,
after starting slightly, with a drawn look.

Their figures were all dully reflected in the little expanse
of water of the basin, but there were water-lilies that hid a
great deal of the great Shodbutt from the bust up, like a
plastron of protrusive vegetation. One lily was plastered like
a mighty sporran upon the centre of his reflection, and his
image trod upon a third.

'I did not know you knew the Crooks.'

'Yes, I know the Crooks very well!' Rhoda Hyman
answered with a painful moon-struck smile (coined in the
ambulatories of the colleges upon the Cam, by the highest
of all highbrows, and her dear master, as he was the master
of so many others, in the deportment of the mind) – inti-
mating of course that it was certainly more likely that *she*

should know a Crook than that the plebeian Shodbutt should know a great hostess of that type and of that name. In fact, Crooks, in the nature of things, not to mention Wellesleys, were more in her line – the aristocratic line of course. For both Shodbutt and Rhoda Hyman were two old sturdy burgesses at heart, say snobs and have done with it if you must indulge in spade-calling: though, because Mrs Hyman was the daughter of a journalist, she had an obvious advantage over the great critic of the *Morning Outcry* – who it is true was a journalist *now*, but had been begot by a village postmaster only, perhaps, or by a genteel West Riding tax-collector maybe, upon a paltry nursery governess or haberdasher's help.

'Ah cher maître!' vociferated the Frenchman, the would-be prize-winner (a new role for him!) making full use at once of all the sentimental advantages of his mother-tongue: 'Comment allez-vous, Monsieur Shodbutt! Il y a longtemps, n'est-ce pas cher maître, depuis que nous nous sommes recontrés. Ça va être bientôt trois ans, n'est-ce pas! Mais si! Mon dieu, que le temps file vite! De jour en jour de plus en plus pressé, pas vrai?' Drawing a deep breath, Monsieur Jolat delivered himself of an appropriate quotation:

> *'Ant att may pack I allvays hee-re*
> *Timeps winkett charr-reeott hurree in nee.'*

'En effet,' said Joan Shodbutt.

'*I* don't hear it, sir!' grinned and growled the great S.S., sturdy and gruff with the Johnson touch, on the 'I smell you in the dark!' model.

'Ah mais alors – un gaillard comme vous! Je comprends! Le temps n'existe pas pour de tels monsieurs, c'est entendu, mon cher Shodbutt!'

'Allons donc! Va! Et pour toi! Sapristi!' exclaimed Shodbutt lightly, tapping Monsieur Jolat in the tummy, and receiving a sharp tap in return.

Rhoda Hyman – who could scarcely suffer the sound of a real live Frenchman in the act of degrading himself – prostituting the prose tongue of Proust and Pascal, employing it to address such a person as Shodbutt – turned away, with a sick look. At this moment Donald Butterboy sprang forward, hissing with excitement:

'Ah, is it Mr Shodbutt! Mr Shodbutt?'

The great Samuel Shodbutt inclined his head.

'I hope you don't object to my introducing myself! I am Donald Butterboy! Yes, yes!' he nodded violently as Shodbutt opened his mouth and raised his eyebrows: 'Donald Butterboy!'

'Ah, Butterboy! How are you?' S.S. gave Butterboy the look that as President of the Book of the Week Club he was accustomed to give to those people, when he happened to meet them, who would wake up one Tuesday morning and find themselves famous (or who had already done so, if he remembered their names).

'Oh *very* well, sir! How – are – *you?*'

'I've read your stuff, Butterboy!'

'Oh please, Mr Shodbutt – don't! Not before all these people!' he hissed in a horror-struck sotto voce.

'What?'

'I know I shall simply blush and go all to pieces if you do – I do feel I've done something most terribly *indecent*. I am heartily ashamed of myself, I really am.'

'Indecent!' Shodbutt frowned. He looked at Joan. 'Is there anything the censor . . . ?'

'No! I mean a book – just *any* book!'

'Oh – ah – not *yours*, Butterboy.'

'Yes! Yes! Yes! *Mine!*'

'Oh! Yours.'

'Mine! Yes I think it is the world's most indecent thing – to write a book.'

Shodbutt looked relieved and Joanie gave a sunny smile.

'Not when you're a genius, Butterboy!' S.S. crashed out and was silent, fixing a frowning eye upon the shrinking lad.

'Yes! Always!' gasped the now thoroughly worked-up Donald.

'Oh, I can't agree with that.'

'I couldn't do it again however much I got, which won't be much, I know. I'm positive I couldn't, however much I tried – not that I *should*, you know!'

Shodbutt looked distinctly shocked.

'It depends what you mean by *much*, Butterboy,' said Shodbutt with a scowl. 'Money's not to be despised! Money's not to be sniffed at, young man. What you don't take, somebody else will!'

'But I *do* appreciate – I am most terribly glad. Money is *everything* – I shouldn't be here, should I, if it wasn't for money?'

'No, you wouldn't,' Shodbutt agreed a little gruffly.

'You said, Mr Shodbutt – you said . . . !'

'I said . . . ?'

'You thought my book was – oh, you can't! – I know it's quite impossible you should but I *do* think it's most terribly kind of you to *say* so – that you do!'

'Your book, Butterboy? It is absolutely first-rate!' crashed Shodbutt fiercely, his bloodshot eye upon the Sévigné-Stavisky Committee, as it were pinning them down. 'I've read it through three times without stopping from beginning to end. Without knowing it I'd got to the end of it – I saw a blank page and I knew it was all over. It's a fact! As sure as I stand here! I should still be reading your book at this minute, over and over again, if my wife hadn't come in and stopped me! And that's another fact! It was only then I found that I was just on the last page – for the *third* time – when she came in and asked me if I wasn't going to bed.

Even then I couldn't put the thing down, I'll be bothered if I could! I took it to bed with me!'

Donald at this became crimson; with an ecstatic jump he screamed at the top of his voice at his illustrious fan —

'Oh, Mr Shod — butt — I am — *flattered* — is-not-the word! If I'd have guessed that you'd taken my little opus *to bed* ...!'

'To bed! Certainly, Butterboy — I give you my word. To bed!'

'To bed! My book ... ! Oh Mr Shodbutt, I have lost my power of speech, I don't know what has happened to me, I really don't!'

'It's the biggest stuff I've read for — for a long time!'

'Oh sir!'

Mr Shodbutt looked straight into the eyes of the great man of the Sévigné-Stavisky Committee who had taken his eyes off Butterboy for a moment, and so had exposed himself to Shodbutt's challenging stare.

'I propose, Butterboy,' snarled Shodbutt slowly, 'I propose to ask my committee to make it next week's BOOK OF THE WEEK!'

'Mr Shod-butt! *Please!* Stop! I cannot bear this all at once, I know I shall faint or something — and perhaps fall in the pond!'

'And I think, Butterboy, you can take it from me — *right now* as our so-called "American Cousins" say — that it *will* be next week's Book of the Week!'

'Mr Shodbutt! How can I thank you! That will be too great an honour — by — *ever so much*!'

Shodbutt (recklessly and glaring very hard at Rhoda Hyman who shrank away, looking back at him in great alarm out of the corner of her eye):

'*No* honour is too great,' the Titan thundered, '*no* honour, for such a work as *It Takes Two to Make a Bedroom-Scene*!'

'Mr Samuel Shodbutt! *How* can I ever thank you? I am dumb.'

'Nonsense, Butterboy.'

'I mean I cannot speak, I'm dumb that way I mean.'

'What next! It's for me, Butterboy, to thank *you*! Believe me, it's *for me*!'

Rhoda Hyman had moved off with the minor light who was with her of Old Bloomsbury Ware towards the house — everyone was turning in that direction.

'Nice, don't you think — but a rather shy boy,' said Joanie as they followed.

Shodbutt nodded.

'Highly strung! Highly strung!' he growled, his eye brooding a little upon the dancing back of next week's genius, who was deep in conversation with the susceptible Scottish parasite-upon-the-libido-of Proust.

Three Press-photographers sprang forward and photographed Shodbutt.

CHAPTER 8

MANY were the sallies made by the great Shodbutt from his place of honour upon the right hand of his American hostess – *nee* Crook – at the expense of the representatives of the Sévigné-Stavisky (*feu* Fémina-Stavisky) Award, of those responsible for the Novel League of Great Britain, the executive of the Genius of the Semester Club, of the Seasonal Award for the Best Mystery Masterpiece, of the Diploma for the Year's Cleverest Literary Larceny (namely Mrs Rhoda Hyman and her co-highbrow), and all the other business rivals and power-competitors he had there – all gathered together upon one spot in a big seething bunch to make them aware of Butterboy (ultimately to 'crown', if that might be, his maiden effort): and the bright-eyed Butterboy sat there upon Mrs Wellesley-Crook's other hand – bashfully playing *peep-bo!* with Shodbutt, first above and then beneath Mrs Wellesley-Crook's bosom, or in the rear of the massive circumference of her bison's head, which she carried like a queen as all American women used to do until they found themselves out.

'I wish you'd sit still, Donald – I know you'll sprain your neck if you go on like that – it's easy to do so and some surgeon will have to put it right for you – I've known that happen and it hurts quite a lot!'

Donald made a wry grimace and placed his manicured fingertips upon his Adam's-apple in genuine alarm.

'Yes that's where it becomes unseated!' his massive protectress assured him.

If Mrs Rhoda Hyman treated Shodbutt as a comic-cut of an ex-best-seller, as he was, if some others (whose bread was buttered on that side, or who were not 'authors' to be injured by the retaliatory lash of Shodbutt's enraged pen) followed that great woman's example – behaving as if Shodbutt had been no more than the most aitchless labourite buffoon in a Socialist Ministry – that was a long way from being the tone adopted by *everybody* towards the great Shodbutt, and Mrs Wellesley-Crook made no end of a fuss of her famous guest. From his vantage-ground at his hostess's side, S.S. stuttered and snarled and struck out at those who had prizes of their own to bestow, and especially such as had kept S.S.'s bossy old finger out of their highbrow literary pie – and at those, too, who pretended that his world-famous mid-page in the *Morning Outcry* should be given to a younger and better man – there were some did that – *he had their numbers*!

Naturally Shodbutt understood that this was an unworthy and spiteful proposal: but there was one thing Shodbutt was adamant about, that was that should he get booted off his Monday-morning pedestal (and the proprietor *had* been shaken latterly once or twice by attacks upon his book-dictator Shodbutt), then Shodbutt had darkly vowed to himself and to Mrs S.S. that 'if younger and better' it must be, then from nothing short of the Infants' Class should his successor be chosen: and that that 'better' should be of a Shodbuttish betterness that should shut out absolutely all that was not second-rate (unless it lived out of England – or was, of course, American, that was understood). Only a bogus *Shodbutt-Made Man* or else a mere Butterboy should be eligible, he would see to *that*! But might that day be far off, naturally, and for the moment the risk was not great, and he was a pretty cocksure dictator as dictators go.

Mrs Rhoda Hyman was a *very* tiresome woman really: there she was as large as life across the table, with her horrid highbrow airs, competing with him, Shodbutt, for the first place. There'd be the *Hades of a row!* muttered Shodbutt to himself (using a favourite locution of his famous weekly book-page — *Hades of a rumpus* sometimes it was) in a minute or two (or as the great critic of the *Outcry* would put it, *in a couple of jiffs*). The wigs would be on the green with a vengeance — he knew he would lose his hair in a couple of shakes! And *then* he told himself there'd be the Old Nick to pay, my word!

Grinning into the Intense Inane, this most egregious of bogus Jane Austens sat over there anyway and ignored Shodbutt — as modestly and with a startled surprise she received the congratulations slavishly offered her for having recently awarded *herself*, out of hand, the Diploma that was in her keeping for the Year's Cleverest Literary Larceny. 'Self-crowned, self-scanned, self-honoured, self-secure!' sneered Shodbutt to himself, remembering a poem by another great critic.

That had indeed been a regal gesture on the part of the Highbrow Queen of Literary London — to 'crown' her *own* work over the heads of all the other works awaiting 'crowns' on the score of bold criminal thefts from other people's books. It was a pale and lovely Cambridge joke (of a mischievous old schoolboy don, uttered in an effaced and tuning-forked falsetto, a manner brought to a great pitch of pleasant inanity by Rhoda) and it had brought the house down in a tempest of giggles. Rhoda gave a one-sided smile of half-thanks.

But with a mooniness almost, of effete demeanour, and with a jagged half-smile all up one side of her narrow face (as faded and wrecked an illumination as was humanly possible, short of that of a corpse-that-sees-the-joke, if that could be), Rhoda Hyman was claiming that she had richly earned the coveted prize by lifting, lock, stock and barrel, a whole chapter from a quite well-known American author (though not so well known in this country – or in New York – as he deserved) and getting away with it.

But at this Shodbutt simply saw red! Ominously he swelled in his place, at the side of his hostess, where there was little room for expansion, too. *That* he would not tolerate! 'Not so well known' – there was no American author, any more, *not so well known in this country as he deserved*, and he would have all the world know that! It was a downright *lie* for Mrs Hyman to say so – and there was, up to the present, no Prize for the Best Lie and he was not going to put up with it! Fair play's a jewel – and if there were at least a dozen prizes for Striking Examples of Foul Play (and he was all for them for his part, being nothing if not go-ahead, else he would not be the progressive person he was) that meant foul play at the expense of everybody except Shodbutt!

No – Mrs Hyman's remark was a deliberate insult levelled at the great critic of the *Morning Outcry*, who could doubt it! Had not Shodbutt for forty years seen to precisely that – that there should be nothing of the sort? And the American reputation followed the Shodbutt-made British, as night the day. So Shodbutt called out:

'Who is that, Mrs Hyman – was I mistaken or did I hear you say that you had stolen from an *American author* for the Cleverest Literary Larceny prize?'

'Yes!' faintly responded the great woman, attacked by the enraged *Epicier* of Letters fairly in the flank, only half turning in his direction, asking herself discreetly what all this could be about.

'An American author *not so well known in America as he deserves?*' the indignant dictator next exclaimed.

'I think so – am I wrong in saying that?' There was a pale and painful smiling on her haggard lips.

'I'm sorry, Mrs Hyman – I am very sorry. But there is *no such American author* in existence!'

'Really.'

'I'm sorry, it's impossible – there is evidently some mistake on your part. The prize has, I am afraid, been bestowed under a misapprehension.'

'I beg your pardon. I have stolen from him in my last book . . .' Mrs Hyman grew a little paler.

'Impossible, my dear lady! Doesn't exist! No such author! None such known to me! Sorry and all that! And that's all about it!'

There was much laughter and a little jeering on both sides, among the onlookers. Butterboy screamed with approval over the bust of Mrs Crook.

'But he does,' faintly insisted the voice of Mrs Hyman. 'He has written a great deal. And – let me assure you of that – he is *damned good to steal from*! I should know – it is not the first time I have done it!'

'His name?'

Mrs Rhoda Hyman (colouring slightly): 'If I am being accused by you, Mr Shodbutt, of *not* having stolen the chapter in question . . .'

'I did not say that! I did not say that!'

'If, in short,' with a fine *pince-sans-rire* assumption of dignity, 'you are impugning my truthfulness . . .'

'Oh no, I believe you as far as that is concerned! You might well have stolen the whole book – but what I said was it *was not from an American author, neglected in his own country*, from whom you pinched it.'

'But I did!'

'Impossible, my dear lady! Thanks to me there is no such person!'

'I am afraid you flatter yourself.'

'Not in this case – I have been known to do it – but not in this case – not in this case!'

(A sly biographical side-glance at his hostess – a look that said 'Mark well how the great man not only "talks for victory", but achieves it', accompanied this, and was duly answered by a look that said 'I marked it well! You scored off that great woman opposite and no mistake!')

'I could name another if I wanted to,' said Mrs Hyman. 'But I am stealing him *next* time. So I will not.'

(And a sickly ghost of sad, sly mirth flickered upon the countenance of Mrs Rhoda Hyman and, departing from it, immediately travelled over the faces of two or three admirers: a delighted titter making its dreary mischievous passage down the table – a bubbling outbreak of faint keen rapture of the donnish variety.)

'I shouldn't, if I were you, keep the name to yourself, Mrs Hyman,' cried Shodbutt scornfully and almost winked at the watching Joanie.

Mrs Rhoda Hyman steadily observed Mr Shodbutt in silence.

'The Americans are not allowed to neglect their authors – I see to that!' Shodbutt blustered, in a paroxysm of boastfulness: 'That is fairly well known I think! They can neglect *ours* if they want to. That's another matter. I don't care about that – we do it ourselves!' He chuckled among his long rabbit teeth. 'But I won't have them neglect *theirs* – and what's more they know it!'

'You bet they do, S.S.!' came a disciple's shrill-chuckling voice from some way down the table.

'No, sir!' S.S. became slightly, truculently, American. 'The Americans haven't neglected an author now for at least six months. Van Shooten was the last. *They'll never do it again!* Since him – none – never!'

'I see,' said Mrs Hyman.

'None. Non possumus! Not possible! Finished! They can't!'

'Very well, Mr Shodbutt – but before you publicly accuse me of dishonesty . . .'

'I did not do that! I did not do that!' S.S. would not have that.

'Or, in fact, of giving myself one hundred pounds sterling for a Literary Larceny I have never committed . . .'

'I never said that! You must not tax me with that!'

'I suggest that you read,' very faintly indeed, 'the works of the novelist in question!'

'Read the works! *An unknown American novelist!* As if there were an American novelist I had not . . .' And Shodbutt turned about him to left and right, as if seeking an unknown American novelist, hidden in the company, he had not spotted.

'Well there is evidently *one* – I'm sorry.'

Shodbutt sneered and it became a little snort, and *il se taisait*, puckering his chin and looking amongst his molars for a missing fragment of meat.

'He also writes essays. They are full of excellent stuff to borrow,' Mrs Hyman persevered.

'Never heard of him!' growled Shodbutt. 'You don't mean Lewis?'

'Sinclair Lewis?'

'Yes – is he your *unknown American novelist*? I made *him* in 1915. Is it Lewis?'

'Oh no, he is fully recognized – owing, I am sure, to you.'

'That is so, of course. I did that. I admit it! I made Lewis!'

'Is it *Wyndham* Lewis?' asked a facetious voice.

There was a very perceptible pause of universal readjustment, at the naming of this Great Unknown nearer home.

Consternation transfixed half of Mrs Hyman's face as this name fell upon her ears, while a faint smirk of secret fun shot up the other half and coloured one of her ears. A titter started down one side of the table, in response to the mirthful half of the highbrow queen's headpiece. Shodbutt's brow was black, it was evident he was displeased – a sucking sound went on amongst his molars.

'No, *not* Wyndham Lewis!' he snarled, and sniffed at the man who had shown such bad taste as to try to be facetious upon such lines as *that*!

'Is it terribly difficult, Rhoda,' asked a very great admirer of Mrs Hyman's novels, 'is it terribly difficult to steal from another writer?'

And the hostess, *née* Crook of Chicago, let out in a long 'Gold Coast' drawl, thickened on purpose, for a special effect:

'I should say,' said she, 'that it must be *technically*, Mrs Hyman, one of the most difficult things to do. I have always admired literary *forgeries* far more than the originals, ever since I was a child. Though I do admire very much indeed a *really* original work, too.'

'It isn't terribly difficult, is it, Rhoda?' asked another of the Hyman *clique*.

'Not really,' said Rhoda. 'It depends.'

'I suppose it does,' said the hostess. 'It must depend. I can realize that.'

'It is the *get away*. Not to be spotted must be half the art,' said a hearty who was a Hyman-fan and coughed.

'That is essential.' Rhoda dispensed all this information with an obvious effort, only, of course, to annoy S.S. who was bursting with eclipsed importance.

'Of course,' slavishly breathed a through-and-through female worshipper, who worshipped herself and all of her sex in this Rhoda Austen of the day.

'It is much more difficult,' said Rhoda Hyman, almost in a whisper, consenting reluctantly to dogmatize, 'to steal, without being detected and denounced, from the living, than to steal from the dead — in spite of the fact that the living are generally speaking more obscure, and usually poor and so unable to defend themselves at law.'

'Oh, much more obscure!' an obscure admirer echoed gladly and wistfully.

But a wrathful sound announced the nature of the feelings of Shodbutt upon this subject — as the word *obscure* assailed his ear.

'I covered up my last theft in a manner worthy of a hero in a book of Van Dine's,' the wicked Rhoda faintly informed the crowd, looking sideways at her crooked hostess.

'Oh, I *do* think Van Dine is marvellous, do you?' shouted three people at once.

'Have you read *The Scarab Murder Case*, Rhoda?' screamed one.

'Do you like Van Dine, Mrs Hyman?' shouted a second.

'There is the most lovely murder in *The Scarab Murder Case*,' screamed a third. 'I have read it — have you?'

'I like a much quieter line in murder,' said Mrs Hyman, 'than Van Dine.'

'And he does write so badly!' an onlooker eagerly agreed all the way up the table.

'Ellery Queen is twice as good!' shouted somebody.

'Stribling is really my man,' said Mrs Rhoda Hyman.

'Is that Young Stribling?' burst out Donald Butterboy, clasping and unclasping his hands beneath the table, and moving restlessly upon his chair in ecstasy.

'Hush, Donald, hush!' thundered his hostess. '*Ta bouche!*'

'Oh, I do think he's too marvellous. After his last fight I went up into his dressing-room — he is far more beautiful stripped – he's even better than he is in the ring, which is saying *a mouthful*. He has a heavenly torso *and* such luscious plump calves. A great smear of blood all across his stomach from the other boxer's nose . . .'

'Hush, Donald!' hissed Mrs Wellesley-Crook with a very severe eye in her head, to the author of *It Takes Two to Make a Bedroom-Scene!* 'You've been drinking!'

'Oh, how *unfair!*' exclaimed Donald. 'I have not touched my glass! But I know quite well what you mean, Maisie, and I think you're horrid, perfectly horrid!'

'How do you mean, you funny boy?'

'You know what I mean quite well, Maisie!' there was a tear in Donald's eye, and his mouth worked convulsively.

'I'm sorry, Donald, you're mad at what I said . . .'

'Who wouldn't be? I knew quite well what you meant, Maisie – that *my nose was red!*'

'Please don't be so *silly*, Donald!'

'I'm not silly, Maisie! I notice you don't *deny* it!'

'Remember, Donald! What did I warn you! Pull yourself together – I'm ashamed of you!'

'Oh, all right, Maisie – I know what you're going to say! But I don't care about the beastly old prize!'

'Donald, you *promised* me. Control yourself! Perhaps you'd better leave the table!'

'No – very well. I'll not open my mouth again.'

The secretary of the Biennial Special Award for the Best Homicide, or Other Crime involving Sudden Death (Fiction or Real Life) – called B.S.A.F.B.H., exclaimed and everyone now turned their attention to him:

'I have just been sent the manuscript of a book by a very promising writer.'

'Oh, who is he, Bob?'

'I don't know. His plot opens with the operations of a clever international literary crook – he lifts book after book and *gets away with it*! I thought of sending it on to you, Mrs Hyman, as I am assured by the person who sends me the MS that it is based on fact.'

'I wish you had. Will you do so?'

'I can't at once, as I think we shall probably be considering it for our next award.'

'What a pity. But I shall get it when it is published.' Rhoda looked startled, to demonstrate how interested she was.

'It is a wonderful piece of writing – I'm not exaggerating. The hero is an author who lives entirely upon thefts of ideas, practically all from the works of one man – a less successful colleague.'

'I knew a man like that,' a lady said.

'So did I,' said Mrs S.S. very civilly.

'But he is also a critic,' said the secretary of the B.S.A.F.B.H. 'His character is also a critic.'

'A critic as well!' said Shodbutt loudly. 'An author and a critic as well?'

'Yes. A very powerful critic.'

'Powerful – ah! Hum. Powerful!' S.S. responded.

'The fact that he is a powerful critic enables him to keep the works from which he steals in constant eclipse. But his own reputation grows daily.'

'Does he review his own books?' Rhoda's second-string eagerly inquired, leaning forward, as if at the play.

'Of course – under assumed names. He reviews his own books sometimes in as many as six different periodicals at once.'

'There is nothing improbable in that,' said a Van Dine fan.

'Nothing,' another enthusiast exclaimed – most of the company turned in his direction for he was a relative outsider. 'There is Geoffrey Bell who is reader for *Hector Golly-*

wog and Ogpu, who in his capacity of novel-critic of the *Sunday Messenger* writes the most glowing accounts of the books that reach him as critic from the firm to which he belongs, as reader.'

There is an interval of smouldering embarrassment after this, broken by a nasty laugh: the enthusiast feels he has been snubbed and coughs, affecting to have swallowed something the wrong way.

S.S. glares dully at him.

'But there seems some danger that the obscure and un-successful milch-cow will dry up,' proceeded the secretary of the B.S.A.F.B.H. 'He writes nothing for eighteen months. The hero is extremely disturbed – it is at that point *we* come in.'

'Ah – the B.S.A.F.B.H.?'

'The B.S.A.F.B.H.! The homicide occurs in connection with the brilliant literary crook's efforts to stimulate his milch-cow.'

'How lovely!' exclaimed several people at once.

'How wonderful!' says Mrs Wellesley-Crook. 'But how does the homicide occur? I don't see how it comes in! Does he kill his milch-cow!'

'Ah, that's the fun.'

'I see. The milch-cow lives.'

'The plot is most intricate. You must read the book, Mrs Wellesley-Crook'.

'I certainly shall.'

At the farther end of the immense table a group of guests had for some time been engaged in a heated discussion as to the particular class to which *Murder at Plenders* belonged, that latest masterpiece by the great Francis Everton. Gladys Mitchell had, among the go-ahead and enlightened, a great following. *Death Traps* had its partisans. At the glorious name of Edgar Wallace (who was now past his peak but still a name to conjure with) a magical and disruptive effect was produced. Soon the entire table was divided into camps, and the old battles about *The Crimson Circle*, *The Yellow Snake*, *The Terrible People*, or *The Squeaker* were fought all over again. One staunch Oppenheimer-fan dashed in with *Algernon Knox: Detective*. Such illustrious names as those of the Coles, of Sayers, of Canon Whitechurch — Anthony Berkely, Cross and Freeman, resounded upon all sides.

But there was one very dark-eyed and fiery young man who, now with the dervish-like fervour of a demented boy scout, insisted over and over again upon the merits of Seltzer's masterpiece — *Square Deal Anderson*.

'*Square Deal Anderson* is a masterpiece!' he thundered. 'It's in the first rank!'

He could be heard from one end of the table to the other. Also he reminded his immediate neighbours of *The Range Boss* and of *The Vengeance of Jefferson Gawne*. But he could obtain no following. His Wild West impulses were respected: but they were not shared by anybody really wholeheartedly. At this he became very aggressive indeed. He asserted with a grating sneer in a voice worthy of his pioneer enthusiasms, that he *might* be very young, and he *supposed* they despised him (and that of course, apart from being so disgustingly young, he was not himself *an author* or anything marvellous of that sort *as yet* — he was nobody — and his passionate boy-scout glances were hurled particularly, it was generally remarked, in the direction of Donald Butterboy) *but* (and he ground his teeth a little) *the time would come* when they would *see*. He knew he was nobody but *some day* he would be as great a man as any people who thought themselves ever so important, just because they scribbled off a lot of stuff about *Bedroom-Scenes* and so forth. But this speech created a very bad impression. And Mrs Wellesley-Crook exclaimed angrily to her guests in general, as if they were all to blame, since they had all been assembled from the same quarter and were responsible for each other she supposed:

'Who is that young man? *Who* brought him here?'

She was told that he was one Osorio Potter and that he was a friend of Donald's at Oxford, and she said to Donald angrily:

'What possessed you, Donald, to bring that stupid boy here with you! He is a very stupid boy. Why did you bring him here?'

But Donald said that Osorio had come of his own accord – he had told Osorio he was coming and Osorio had said he would come along too, he couldn't help it – Osorio followed him everywhere and he just couldn't shake him off.

'But he says the most horrible things about you, Donald darling, and seems to dislike you *very much*! He is a dangerous young man. I should say very dangerous.'

And Donald said *Yes* – that was so, Osorio *did* hate him terribly and loathe him utterly, but that it didn't matter. And Maisie said:

''M well. I think it *does* matter. And if he doesn't behave himself I shall tell him to go back to Oxford.'

But Donald smiled and said that Osorio would never do it, he wouldn't dream of going back to Oxford.

'Oh wouldn't he!' said Maisie Wellesley-Crook. 'You think he wouldn't!'

'I'm positive he wouldn't!' Donald said, very pleased indeed.

There were two people who had taken no part in the fast and furious debate as to which was the greatest writer, Edgar Wallace or one of the many other famous crime-kings. One of them was Shodbutt.

It is true that Shodbutt never wrote detective-stories. But he *had* written, years ago, detective-stories. What about *The*

Grand Ritz-Plaza Splendide – what was that? and was it not about time somebody remembered the fact? Also, Shodbutt could not forgive Edgar Wallace, whom in the old days he had known quite well, those gigantic royalties, those staggering six-figure sales. Edgar Wallace made him feel small in a way that no mere Henry James, no highbrow-stylist, however great his following, could: and Edgar Wallace was to Shodbutt a red rag to a bull in a china shop.

At first intimidated, Shodbutt sat silent, but when his hostess asked him what *he* had to say to these crime-kings of equal honour both in Life and Letters, he stuttered and stumbled: he '*took off his hat* to Edgar Wallace – Edgar Wallace,' he said, 'was a bright lad, a bright lad!' But all that he could answer to the rest of this *kermesse* of Red Crime was that he had read Emile Gaboriau again the other day, and *he took his hat off to him – Gaboriau was a genius!* (He had not said Edgar Wallace was *a genius* – he had merely 'taken off his hat' to Edgar Wallace – he felt some queer compunction about employing the word 'genius' where E.W. was concerned, he did not know why!)

'I first read *L'Affaire Lerouge* when I was ten. I read it last week. It is a masterpiece!' He felt at home at once with Gaboriau – all the usual words tripped back to his tongue. 'It is as much better than *The Squeaker* as Jane Austen is better than – well *out-of-sight* better than a certain lady, who is as a matter of fact not sitting so very far away from us at this moment!'

'Oh!' said Mrs Wellesley-Crook, delighted. 'You don't mean Mrs Rhoda Hyman, do you by any chance, Mr Shodbutt?'

It was certainly Mrs Rhoda Hyman that the great Shodbutt had meant. He half-winked at his imposing hostess and chuckled in his denture, chiselled out of cheese-rind, and under cover of his dripping moustache secreted a sly smile of elephantine malice.

'*L'Affaire Lerouge,*' he said ponderously, 'has plot, it has structure, poise, firmness, coolness, clearness, boldness. *It is a work of genius!*'

And he left no doubt at all as to this being meant equally to apply to Gaboriau or Austen, as against Wallace or Hyman.

But the other man who took no part in this inevitable discussion, which occupied almost the whole of lunch, was a gentleman who was sitting beside Baby Bucktrout. (Upon the other side of Miss Bucktrout was Osorio Potter.) This silent, smiling gentleman listened, however, to Osorio's remarks about Seltzer, and he evidently relished them very much indeed. But he did not say so: he did not open his mouth. It was apparent that he was no crime-fan. And when luncheon at length came to an end he followed Osorio out and took his arm in a curious smiling intimate way, that was paternal and brotherly at once.

'My dear boy,' he said, 'how I admire your stand!'

'My what?'

'Your bold stand – for the Lone Gulch School of Literature!'

CHAPTER 9

WHEN the train had drawn out of the station, the platform of which he had left vibrating with his dramatic roar of 'MURDERER', Osorio, or Ossie for short, had immediately fallen asleep. The whole unwarranted and somewhat ungentlemanly call made upon his intellect, as well as the emotional strain entailed, in his heated conversation with Charlie, had taken it out of him, and he needed rest. So sleep came to him at once, with a tropical suddenness – if one may so express oneself about a human person, and a stolid British lad.

When, half an hour later, he woke up Osorio had left behind the Secret Service atmosphere of objectionable highbrow crime. All that baffling world of masonic police thugs, who spoke a language he could not understand full of *weeing* and *vooing*, of complicated mystically-minded spadassins, which old Charlie had gossiped of with such an easy familiarity, was a thing of the past. He had put a solid cement of good sound sleep between himself and all that. He breathed freely again. He gazed out, like any simple-hearted cracksman or modern Dick Turpin upon the grim pastures of Old England.

By Secret Service tales he had always been repelled. The nearest he had ever come to that had been when a very sophisticated friend of his at Oxford had been the cause of his agreeing to read *The Hairless Mexican*, and other stories in a big book he didn't like at all. *The Hairless Mexican* he liked because it was about a Mexican, and as a reader he was pretty familiar with the Mexican border. He was at home with Mexicans. But the mere word 'spy' in a book was quite enough anyway to make him put it down and label it a dud. As to the War, *that* he definitely hated. It was a period where homicide was so common that the soul of both crook and sleuth must shrivel up, at the mere thought of it – crime and 'fiction' was so put in the shade by such a thing that it must lose its very meaning. And he was all for Crime, and not at all for War. As a tiny tot he had heard the big bangs and seen the silver Zepps but they meant nothing to him – that was an alien world into which he had been born. No more of that for him, thank you – it was as great a bore as a history book. Ypres was a name like Flodden Field. 'Kaiser Bill' was cheek by jowl in his mind with Barbarossa.

The 'Lone Gulch School of Literature' was his favourite reading certainly; although his championship of it just now had been rather an act of bravado than an involuntary expression of a burning faith. He had been impelled by some, as it were, crusading impulse to insist upon it, in the company in which he found himself. For the attitude to Crime of some of these penmen and literary ladies (all of whom he most heartily disliked) had upset him very much, and more than one had definitely put his back up. His feelings could be best expressed (it was discovered by his very exacerbated Subconscious) by going over, in full view of the company, and planting himself defiantly upon the side of the neglected 'Lone Gulch School', in a way he had never thought of doing before. His affinities were made manifest, even dimly to himself, *as never before*. He had felt just like a 'bad man' of the prairies among a lot of kid-glove crooks, with their crowd of high-hatting Molls all joining-in the palaver – so obviously high-school girls to the hennaed finger-nails as to just turn a poor, honest 'bad man' queasy and in short make him feel real *bad*. And Osorio had detected in himself almost a desire to draw his gat and shoot at the electric lights in their sconces, 'drilling' perhaps a footman or two in the general confusion that would ensue. And as to the spectacle of Donald Butterboy, that had in itself been far more than sufficient to put him beside himself – Donald, smirking and mincing, proudly installed beside the impressive hostess, as the little lion of the occasion, and himself at the extremity of the table, so that he had to shout to be heard at the centre of things, with no place in the sun at all!

So now for some time, after his outburst, Osorio sat with the silent gentleman – who upon closer acquaintanceship was seen to be quite garrulous – in a secluded corner: not so secluded as the latter could have wished, but still out of earshot of any but the most sharp of hearing.

The silent gentleman's name was, oddly enough, Sir Titus L'Estrange: he was a neighbouring squire of sorts, of a strange sort indeed, but friendly with all the Crooks. Sir Titus was a knight of Saint Michael and Saint George, an ex-governor of an Asiatic British Crown Colony, of course tanned, but clean-shaven, with a mouth denoting iron will – an iron will *to please*. The discerning would have little doubt, as they marked his bright and restless eye, that he possessed all the vices of the East as well as his fair share of its sunburn. There was a monocle, it was the only monocle in the party except that of Lady Saltpeter (who was not present) – whose contemporary Sir Titus was quite one of the naughtiest of her Nineties' co-culprits. He pinched Osorio's arm, who showed the effect of the pain by a grimace and shook Sir Titus off with a scowl.

'Did I hurt you, Osorio? May I call you Osorio?'

'Why not?'

'I can see no objection.'

'Absolutely none, except that I don't know who you are and don't care!'

'You are a big muscular fellow, Osorio – I shouldn't like to meet you alone on the *sierra* on a windy night and for it to be your life or mine!'

'How do you know I'm muscular?'

'Because I felt your punching arrangement, stupid.'

'Did you? Well, leave it alone in future, do you hear!'

'Of course.'

'You ought to be ashamed of yourself! How did you get in here?'

'I don't know. How did you, come to that!'

Osorio went out into the garden and Sir Titus followed him.

'Osorio!'

'Oh, are you still there? What is it now?'

'Nothing much. I'm a fresh-air snob. Like yourself I like the great open spaces. I thought I'd move into the garden.'

'Is that all?'

'Did you notice me at lunch?'

'I can't say I did.'

Sir Titus looked a little pained.

'Unkind!'

'No. One doesn't notice gentlemen in white spats.'

'Indeed! If I had known I'd have left them at home.'

'One only sees people of one's own age, I find.'

'How dull.'

'Dull perhaps for *you*, sir!'

Osorio returned into the hall. He went into a large room full of books and searched for a volume of the Lone Gulch School but could see nothing but biographies of Winston Churchill and Lord Morley. Sir Titus was with him.

'I notice that all the children are still discussing their favourite thrillers,' said Sir Titus.

'I know I am *young* – you needn't remind me of that!'

exclaimed Osorio Potter with great heat. 'But I'm not ashamed of it.'

'But we're *all* young today, Osorio – look at us!'

'I *have* looked at you.'

A burly stranger in strange tweeds, of outlandish if not outmodish cut, approached and said to Sir Titus:

'Sir Titus L'Estrange?'

'Yes,' said Sir Titus. 'I am Sir Titus L'Estrange.'

'I don't suppose you remember me, I am Richard Dritter.'

'Of course I do!'

'Was it not in '97 that we last met – in Venice, yes, it was in Venice!'

'Venice – so it was! How are you, my dear Dritter!'

Osorio Potter was leaving them.

'Please, Osorio,' said Sir Titus, 'you need not go away – it is very discreet of you but neither Mr Dritter nor myself are likely to wish to be alone to discuss our Venetian memories, we have nothing to hide, either of us!'

'Speak for yourself!' cried Dritter in a great roguish Ninetyish voice, and with a high-hearted Ninetyish cackle: 'Speak for yourself!'

'This is Richard Dritter, the great painter.'

Osorio Potter with some condescension turned back at the word 'painter' and consented to be presented to Dritter. Artists often played quite prominent parts in the unravelling of crime. Many detectives were amateur painters.

'How do you do?' he said quite affably for him.

'I have never listened,' said Richard Dritter, 'to so much talk about sleuths and clues, and bloodstained axes and false beards, *never*!'

And as he said 'false beards' the burly Dritter laughed uproariously in his own enormous coarse grey beard as-if-it-had-been-false; and as he saw Osorio Potter's eyes upon it (for Osorio wondered if Dritter were *disguised* and he was examining the place where the beard ended and the face began) he laughed again, with weighty German heartiness, which would have pulverized anyone less arrogant than Osorio, and less equal to every emergency than Sir Titus.

'One must draw the line somewhere,' said Sir Titus, 'and I refuse to talk all day long about *detectives*. Police constables are another matter – they are a fine body of men, that is different.'

'Aren't they! Ah well – by their *livres de chevet* shall you know a generation!' said Dritter. 'Edgar Wallace! It is not asking much of life, Edgar Wallace – a poor little humble taste! We are modest today, are we not?'

'Their tastes are humble: but *they* are not humble!' And Sir Titus beamed at Osorio, with his brow of a schoolboy paladin.

'The Paris Commune for a political model precludes humility,' shouted Dritter with gusto. 'And with Samuel Shodbutt as your Sainte Beuve, you must expect Edgar Wallace to become your Gustave Flaubert.' And Dritter laughed again, softly this time – softly lest it trod on his dreams.

Osorio Potter had been turning away, but as he heard the name of Shodbutt a fierce light came into his handsome buccaneering eyeballs and he changed his mind and remained.

'What do you think of Shodbutt?' he asked the great painter. 'He is an old fool, isn't he?'

'Certainly.'

'What do you think of the Book of the Week Prize? It is absurd, I think.'

'I agree with you entirely,' said Dritter. 'It is worse than absurd. It is obscene.'

'I am glad you think so,' said Potter. 'I have always been sure that it was a prize for the worst book ever, as I am quite sure otherwise that Donald Butterboy wouldn't be given it.'

'It is preposterous spoof, of course.'

'As bogus as anything could be!' exclaimed Potter fiercely.

'Bogus describes it perfectly,' Dritter promptly replied.

Osorio grew almost cordial. This old fellow in a false beard was a decent sort he thought. He wished the other would go away. Richard Dritter, shooting a tactful glance from under his bushy brows at Osorio, recognized that he had struck a congenial note and pleased the young man, who was evidently waiting for more of the same sort.

'Shodbutt as a best-seller is one thing,' he consequently went on, 'but Shodbutt as a Weekly Dictator of Letters — coming to awful decisions as to what is good, and what is bad, what shall live and what shall die, in every province of creative literature — that is another. It is charlatanry of the worst sort.'

'That's what I think!' Potter shouted loudly. 'Charlatan!'

'Only in such a time as this could you get a man of Shodbutt's calibre assuming importance — at any other time such a thing would be impossible.'

'That's what I think — why is it he is so important?'

'He suits the book — he suits the Book of the Week book shall I say — of the commercial newspaper gentlemen who employ him! Books are big business, Mr Potter — you must realize that!'

'I suppose they are,' said Osorio, somewhat depressed: the word *business* always depressed him.

'Still he's a blackguard!' cried Dritter noisily, guffawing a great deal in his beard.

Osorio was delighted.

'He should be shown up!' he cried. 'The man should be shown up at once!'

'Of course he should – but we're all a pretty tame lot these days!'

'I don't call *Osorio* tame!' Sir Titus archly intervened, in a thrilling bray – seesawing archly upon the syllables of Os-or-io.

'No, of course Shodbutt's weekly-genius business is fantastic humbug, we all know that,' Dritter pursued. 'He's intelligent enough to understand as much himself. Shodbutt knows he is playing the intellectually destructive game of the commercial philistine. But after all he *is* a philistine himself. There's no getting away from that!'

'Philistine!' snorted Potter, wondering what the Old Testament or anything to do with church had to do with the subject in hand.

'Shodbutt belongs to the trash-bin he serves, no one can deny it! Its values are, all said and done, *his* values. So there you are. Still he's an old ruffian, he's a wicked old ruffian, I'm afraid, young man. As we get older we get *worse*!' And again Dritter shook with laughter.

'Old ruffian,' Potter repeated scornfully. 'I could find a better word for him than that.'

'Why does not somebody get up and denounce him? Why do we all put up with him so meekly?' Dritter asked as if it had just occurred to him, all eagerness for action.

'Why, indeed?' exclaimed Potter. 'I shall denounce him tonight. At dinner!'

'I wish you would!' said Dritter, slapping the thigh of his oddly tweed-clad legs, and, his mouth hollowed out in the midst of his bristling beard, emitting a prolonged high-pitched clownish wail of mirth.

'I'm going to – you see!'

'*Somebody* should have the gumption to prick that bubble – but it's really not worth while. I should leave it alone if I were you.'

'Yes, Osorio,' Sir Titus counselled him, 'prick people of your own age!'

'I shall do nothing of the sort!' said Osorio hot-temperedly. 'Mind your own business.'

'I was after all, Osorio, only advising you to mind yours. Shodbutt is not *your* business. Why doesn't Dritter challenge him if he feels so strongly about it?'

'But it's not my business either!' Dritter protested noisily, with much gesticulation, of a heavily gallic order: 'It's no business *whatever* of mine! How could it be? I am a painter. It's the business of the writers to do it – we don't call in *novelists* to demolish our art-critics for us – we dip our largest hogshair brush in a juicy mixture of *Terre de Siene* and other excremental shades of pigment, and give them a biff in the eye with it – when they come too much of it!'

Sir Titus smiled a grim approval of his illustrious contemporary, who, having shot his bolt, passed on, waving adieu to the regretful Osorio; in this immensely distant age-class, buried in a vast false-beard, and disporting himself in a swashbuckling manner of such studied suavity-begot-upon-spectacular-vigour as made Potter's swashbuckling appear an opposite genus, he had been unexpectedly revealed as a kindred soul to the redoubtable youth. As with a slight la-de-da stagger of his ponderous limbs, in the outsize Tchecko-slovak tweeds, with parting explosions of the heartiest and most theatrical Ninetyish fun in his *pastiche* chin-ornament, Dritter moved off, Sir Titus turned to Osorio and said:

'I like Dritter, don't you?'

'Yes – why has he left us?'

'How should I know! He was reputed to be the most brilliant talker of all those gathered about Oscar.'

'Oscar?'

'Yes – a very intelligent man who lived long ago and came to a very sticky end.'

'Oh. Yes, Dritter seems a good talker. Does he always talk like that?'

'I expect so, it amuses him. He is a painter, of course, but like his master, Whistler, he has a tongue to his credit as well as a brush.'

'Whistler?'

'Yes.'

'Who was that?'

'A painter, too, like Dritter – a small man with hair dyed black, all but a white lock. Also with a goatish tuft upon his saucy Yankee chin.'

'Oh.'

Osorio left him quickly, in the direction taken by Dritter.

CHAPTER 10

MONSIEUR JOLAT, in the baronial hall become a bustling lounge, led Mr Shodbutt up and down. He held him by the arm: directing the lovely mother-tongue which he shared with Stavisky, Malvy, Bony and many thousands more of the French *élite* into the ears of Shodbutt, he listened for the spasmodic '*en effets!*' that issued, in response, from the great critic's bristling, snarling, mouthpiece. Up and down they went, in an imposing dawdle, like doctor with rich convalescent patient; or very talkative man-nurse, say, with his grinning elderly charge: or – equally well – like a successful engineer showing off his model robot. Certainly *showing off* was well in progress, and likewise a lot of coaxing and caressing was going on; and decidedly the Shodbutt model was on the monosyllabic side. It required a great deal of stimulation, and it got it.

Negotiating corners, the solicitous Frenchman was at pains to see that his precious exhibit should not get knocked, or get its legs crossed: in this way as they were about to pass through the door leading into the vestibule of the library beyond (in which stood large plaster busts of the 'book-world' of a past age – Dryden, Donne, Chaucer, Swift, and the rest, 'geniuses' of an antiquated type, who admittedly would have no chance today) Jolat and Shodbutt became transfixed for a short while – but this was because Shodbutt had desired Monsieur Jolat to pass first – *toujours la politesse* – and stopped at a moment when he shouldn't, as a good machine: and Monsieur Jolat, misunderstanding the motive of the sudden halt, had attempted to drag him through. At this, resolved not to be outdone in politeness in the public eye, Shodbutt had backed: but Monsieur Jolat, to counteract this unexpected movement and remove the unfortunate hitch, had dragged upon him with the full weight of his Escoffieresque breadbasket, so that it became a sort of tug-of-war. A dead stop was the result. At length neither passed through the door properly – both returned into the lounge, Shodbutt still crowing 'C'est à toi de passer le premier!' and Monsieur Jolat vociferating 'Mais jamais! *Jamais!*' – for Shodbutt was of course as obstinate as a mule in politeness as in everything else. If he was not the First Gentleman in Europe he was in the running and he did not propose to be displaced by a second-rate Frenchman – so he pulled with a will and put his back into it when asked to go through the door first.

Now at the hands of women of the sort of Mrs Hyman, well-to-do donnish middle-class women, Shodbutt had had to suffer a lot, especially at the hands of one: but that was not the only sort of woman whose contentious shadow fell across the rose-strewn path of the great book-dictator. Stella Salt was a very different kettle of fish to Rhoda Hyman: she had none of the latter's economic, and thereby social, advantages; and Shodbutt would certainly never spend a sleepless night over old Stella. Yet she was a gadfly that had now and then succeeded in vexing him; and with this great feminist authoress he had many a quiet passage of arms, both in the Press and out of it.

Stella Salt sat now and observed, from a table where she drank her coffee with a couple of women admirers, the oscillations of Shodbutt, in his deliberate, ponderous, passage back and forth; and as she watched him she decided that this would be a propitious moment to deliver an attack – a little extempore skirmish: for his loftily-cocky frown, and his conceited paunch, corseted and fobbed, annoyed her. She rose, and leaving her friends went to meet this perambulating Entente Cordiale, as it slowly rolled along in her direction – perhaps more like the 'Russian steam-roller' of wartime Press messages than the political child of Edward the Peacemaker.

Stella was a big old girl, very determined looking, with an easy platform-manner and a beefy swing of the arm. She was a somewhat greying golden blonde, with an amusing feline face, who in her time had hungerstruck with the best and trumpeted the slogans of democratic revolt and red feminine revolution. Born not so very far away from where Shodbutt had seen the light, her blood possessed the same black-country aggressiveness and grim grit. The thick amber rims of her spectacles enclosed two darkling eyes, and her mouth now took on a flower-like curl for the discharging of a taunt.

'Being taken for a constitutional!' she began as he approached.

'Something of the sort, Stella. Something of the sort!' croaked the great man.

Monsieur Jolat slowed them down and politely came to a halt – although Shodbutt's legs, in independence, still had a restless forward movement, suggestive of a desire to proceed on the part of their master.

'Why are we all gathered here, S.S.? Have you found out, or are you as much in the dark as the rest of us?'

'I'm in the dark,' chuckled S.S. 'Can't make it out at all. There does seem to be an *embarras de richesse*, doesn't there?'

'It can't be that we've all been brought down here to see – what's his ridiculous name?'

'Whose? Crook?'

'No, uncle – *not* Crook! You know very well who I mean – I saw you with him just now!'

'I've met so many people here – I didn't particularly want to . . . !'

'I have it – I mean Butterboy. That's it. Butterboy I meant.'

'Oh, young Butterboy!' Shodbutt frowned. Stella meant to be tiresome, it was but too plain. His chin puckered – he made a cocky sucking sound in his cheek. 'We might have displaced ourselves on account of somebody far worse than Donald Butterboy!' Samuel Shodbutt growled – who had not relished 'uncle' – especially from Stella – and was working himself up: the iteration of the name of his protégé had the effect of an incantation upon him – he swelled and became the weekly dervish of his routine tirade in his renowned book-page. 'Donald Butterboy is not *le premier venu*, Stella, not Donald Butterboy. By a long chalk.'

'Isn't he? I'm glad to hear that!' sneered Stella. Shodbutt went on swelling visibly – Monsieur Jolat was compelled to move away an inch or two to make room.

'It's no use, Stella. You're wrong this time! Donald is *the goods*!'

Stella Salt, with a sleek sneer all her own, looked the great Shodbutt *dans le blanc des yeux*. These two were very old acquaintances, from before the flood. She had known him at a time when far from being a dictator or anything imposing of that sort, he was a respectable, high-class best-seller, with, as a side-line, a small and rather select reputation as a critic of good books and good books only. He was laboriously building up, in those distant days, a stern little incorruptible critical reputation, in a left-wing periodical with a fairish minority circulation, in which she was pegging away as well.

So she knew this shoddy sunset of blustering verbiage from A to Z, she saw perforce this tartuffian betrayal for what it was, the bombast of a buffoon, since she had been an eye-witness of the honest if dull noontide of ill-paid hard work. She was expert enough to understand that this full-blooded imperial purple was but a thin suffusion at the best, an optical phenomenon of decline, before the plunge – and even so only made possible by a life-time of mediocre industry. By keeping straight for *three* decades, Mr Samuel Shodbutt had been able to sell out that asset, honesty (for which there is always a market, however little may be its intrinsic value), and so enable himself to be spectacularly crooked for *one* – the *last*. An achievement even that, in its kind: but largely an accident of the history of book-production, and of the happy fact that Shodbutt was there at the moment of the transition to the mass-produced book: due, too, to the rich manure of gold, poured out by the Book-magnates from their banks to dye and flood-light the whole firmament of the literary world a cheap red – with this bogus glow to mask the death of culture – so that it was easy to deafen the welkin with the sham bluffness of this small, vastly-inflated apostate, Shodbutt – that unpretentious and painstaking little reviewer as Stella had known him of the Edwardian literary backwater, dominated by Shaw and by Wells.

She knew her Shodbutt *à fond*, beyond a cavil, and so he, beneath this taunting third degree, of reminiscent eyes, shuffled about continually, though he would not say to Jolat, 'Let us move on!' He stood his ground, after an uneasy fashion. However, he wound up his snarl, and he fixed a lacklustre eye upon Miss Stella *too* – turning over tartly in his mind all the things he knew about *her*, and counted his ammunition.

'Donald Butterboy is not *le premier venu*!' he exclaimed again as Stella said nothing, preferring an eye-attack to a tongue-attack – fixing her gaze upon the restless freckled eyes, whose melancholy jauntiness was suffering beneath her regard.

'En effet!' burst in Monsieur Jolat. 'Il n'est *pas* le premier ve-*nu*! Ah ça non! Je m'en garantie. C'est un garçon qui est assez bien foutu, celui-là! Ma foi, oui! Il est bougrement talentueux! Il est bien loin d'être le premier ve-*nu*, mademoiselle! Si nous en avions deux ou trois en France de cette taille-là, eh bien, nous aurions à nous feliciter, mademoiselle! – Il n'est *pas* le premier ve-nu!'

Stella laughed.

'It sounds better in French, doesn't it!' she said. Shodbutt shrugged his shoulders.

'But have we really been asked to come all this way, S.S., to observe this prodigy?'

'You are too bitter, Stella. Too bitter altogether.'

'Is it *bitter* to ask why so many literary personages have been assembled here – unless perhaps it is because of what Monsieur Jolat here would call their *beaux yeux*?'

Monsieur Jolat saw his opportunity – the gallic graces became à propos, nay were imposed on him, by the casual use of this French cliché.

'Ah, mademoiselle! I would haf come far farther, believe me, than Bum-men-den for eyes far less *beaux* than your own!'

Stella bowed.

'Sir,' she said, 'you have the gallantry of your nation.'

She was rather pleased – but Shodbutt looked *moqueur* – the slight relaxation of her face had given him his chance, too.

'How about *my* eyes, Jolat?' he stammered, in one of his most vexing high-pitched snarls. 'How about *my* eyes after all?'

'I believe Mr Shodbutt is right,' Stella retorted. 'We have all been asked down here to look at *his* eyes. How stupid of me! – that is obviously what this party must have been for!'

'May not the male have *eyes* as well?' came Shodbutt's staccato croak.

'I suppose we shall all end up by being present at the prize-giving,' Stella continued, 'when he hands over the Book of the Week Club trophy, and we shall be expected to clap our hands off. I can see how this will end!'

'Well, why not, why not!' argued Shodbutt cockily and gaily – well on top, he felt, and going strong. 'It will do you good, Stella, to have to clap somebody else's work for a change – even if he *is* so young. It's not *a sin* to be young, Stella!'

'Sometimes it is – as it is sometimes a sin to be old!'

'The young are not to be despised, Stella, my girl – we old fogies mustn't be too stiffnecked about it if we are given a back seat and told to *clap*.'

'Despised! Who said they were, you old humbug?'

'We all know it's a case of sour grapes, Stella! We all know it's a bad case of sour grapes!'

'Sour grapes! What do you mean by that?'

'I knew you were angry with me, Stella!'

'Why?'

'Because I gave it to young Margery Mendel instead of to your book, you know – it was rough luck and I was sorry but I can't give it to everybody! I can't go on giving it to my old friends!'

'What is *it* in heaven's name! Are you talking about your precious weekly book-prize by any chance?'

'That was what I had in mind,' grinned the horrid Shodbutt toothily.

'Well, I wouldn't have the beastly thing at any price, and that is *not* a case of sour grapes, believe me! If you really wanted to insult me you would offer me *that*!'

'Wait till I do, Stella darling – wait till I do!'

'You grow weak-minded, that is evident. Have you really taken *yourself* in with all that ballyhoo!'

'Well, let's be toddling along, Jolat. Stella will be scratching my *beaux yeux* out in a minute, I'm afraid. She's a devil when she's roused is Stella!'

'Yes, you'd better move about a little! Lead "our greatest critic" away, Monsieur Jolat – march him up and down a little longer, so that everyone may admire the stately vessel of God's literary judgment!'

Thereupon the Entente Cordial took its leisurely departure and Stella drew off, already revolving in her mind the terms of the return match. And for Monsieur Jolat this was all very baffling and disagreeable, of course. As soon as he conveniently could he led the great columnist of the *Morning Outcry* out into the garden, with a sly glance for the militant Stella (which he hoped Shodbutt did not see) who stood hurling her abuse like a biblical harridan planted in the midst of the committee for the Novel League of Great Britain and three prominent members of the senior I.N.K. Club.

But through the door that Monsieur Jolat and the great Shodbutt had just negotiated came an uproar; and then the startled phalansteries and the abashed literary sects beheld the bulging form of Corse, and beneath her arm the writhing form of Baby Bucktrout, dressed in tennis-shorts and a polo-vest.

'You old swine! Let me go!' bellowed the wriggling Bucktrout.

'I won't have you goin' into that there Tool House!' answered Corse, as she advanced, ignoring the great throng of guests.

'I shall go to the Tool House if I want to!' Baby shouted downwards at the ground.

'Not while I'm here, Miss Baby!' answered Corse.

'Which won't be long!' stormed the convulsive Baby. 'Consider yourself as *sacked*!'

'That's as it may be, Miss Baby!'

And they disappeared through a baize swing-door.

CHAPTER 11

In a disused nursery in the South Wing of Beverley Chase, Baby Bucktrout, Osorio Potter, Donald Butterboy, and Corse were assembled. The disused nursery was used as a library and study for any adolescents who might be in the Chase. Corse stood before the door, her arms akimbo. Baby glared at her from a chair upon which she had just sat down. Donald was combing his hair in a looking-glass. Osorio stood between Corse and Baby Bucktrout.

'I shall give Tom the benefit of my company if I want to!' cried Baby Bucktrout. 'I offered him my hand this after-noon – is not that respectable?'

'Respectable! I never heard of such a thing!' growled the lusty Corse.

'I don't suppose you have. But I shall continue to break down Tom's country shyness in any way that occurs to me. You hear?'

'Not if I know it!' snapped the dragon at the door and closed her mouth with a click of sturdy artificial teeth.

'You won't stop me!' clamoured Baby. 'You see if you do.'

'We'll see about that!' responded the grim Corse. 'What can Mister Donald think of you, I wonder? I should think you would be ashamed of yourself.'

'I shall kiss Tom if I want to!'

Osorio's dark and piercing eyes were flashing with anger.

'Does Tom want you to kiss him?' asked Osorio in a very sombre tone indeed.

'What's that got to do with it – what business is it of

yours anyway?' Baby turned upon Osorio with indignation.

'That's not an answer to my question!' stormed Osorio, his voice eclipsing that of Corse.

'I didn't say it was!'

'Yes you did, Miss Baby!' she was contradicted by the female police.

'Oh you *enfants terribles*!' called Donald fretfully from his mirror. '*Thoo* be quiet!'

Donald held with a trembling hand a long pale hair that was a far paler whisky-green than those about it: and he was positive that it was in reality *white*. He gazed at it with horror. Gently he compelled it upwards and then gave it a mild pull. But every time he tweaked it, as he did so shutting his moistened eyes with anticipated pain, it hurt. After a dozen attempts he let it fall, bathed in a cold perspiration.

'This young gentleman's quite right. No lady would behave as you do!' said Miss Corse. 'You ought to be thoroughly ashamed of yourself!'

'Hear, hear!' Osorio said. 'She ought to be.'

'Oh, shut up you!' said Baby.

'It's not your place, Miss Baby, in the Tool House! You can't get round that, for all your book-learning!'

'No, why should you go into the Tool House?' Osorio asked fiercely. 'What do you want there?'

'It's not *your* Tool House!' Baby said.

'Perhaps not!'

'Well, why can't you mind your own business? I don't interfere with *you*!'

'You should have more self-respect!' Corse told her.

'It's for gentlemen only,' said Osorio. 'The Tool House. It's not your province, is it? Miss Corse is right. You have no business there. It's for gardeners, not girls!'

'I shall go where I like. This is my house.' To Osorio, 'You are impertinent.'

129

'I'm not your servant! I'm not Miss Corse.'

'What are you doing here anyway, I should like to know?'

'I am here with your fiancé, as you know. I am his best man. As such I speak.'

'I like that! "Best man." Best man *indeed*.'

'I am your fiancé's friend.'

'Fiancé! That!'

Osorio undulated himself to achieve the most conventional indignation he could muster at such short notice.

'Fiancé, yes. There is no occasion to insult my friend either!' he blustered. 'I won't stand for that. Not as a best man.'

'Is *he* in your charge as well!'

'As a matter of fact I should be sorry to see a friend of mine married to a girl who — well, does what you do in the Tool House!' Osorio acted a turning-on-the-heel, but he did not move away, but stood in profile in expectation of the retort.

'How do you know what I do in the Tool House? Have you ever been in the Tool House?' Baby asked him so pointedly that Miss Corse frowned in the direction of Osorio, to learn what this new subject of dispute might portend.

'Yes, I *have* been in the Tool House.' Osorio hesitated, looking over at Corse. 'I was in the Tool House ten minutes before you, as a matter of fact.'

'Oh, you were, were you?'

'Certainly.'

'And what pray, Mr Potter, were you doing in other people's Tool Houses if I may be allowed to inquire?'

Osorio (with great heat): 'That's my business! That is no one's business but my own.'

'For a guest you take a good deal on yourself, don't you?' Miss Corse took a step forward.

'The young gentleman's quite right to go into the Tool House. I expect he went there to look at the tools. All boys are interested in tools.'

'Well, I won't have him going into the Tool House, that's all about it – he must keep out of it!' cried Baby Bucktrout, very red and angry. 'He has no business there! He's only here on sufferance – Donald says himself he didn't want him to come but couldn't help himself. I shall give orders to Mr Jaspers to throw him out of the Tool House if he finds him there!'

'Babs, *do* be quiet!' howled Donald, who, having lost sight of the hair for a time, now had it firmly by the roots, his eyes choked with water. 'You're insulting my guest!'

'Oh, very well!' said Baby. 'You'd better take your guest away if you don't want me to insult him! I've had about enough of your best man.'

The papercover French edition of *Lady Chatterley's Lover* lay upon the table beside Baby Bucktrout. She seized it and sprang up, holding it tight like a big school book against her hip, and said:

'I'm going to read! You may go now, Corse – I shan't want you any more just yet.'

Baby walked, with a great deal of movement, her buttocks in unjustifiable relief, to an armchair in the farther corner of the room, by a wide open window. Opening *Lady Chatterley's Lover*, she began reading, her face turned to the garden, away from Osorio and Corse.

'Will you promise me, Miss Baby, not to go to the Tool House the moment my back is turned?' asked Corse.

'Certainly not! I shall go to the Tool House the moment you have gone.'

'Oh, you will, will you?'

'Yes. I am not a child. When will you learn that, Miss Corse?'

'You are worse than a child!' said Corse. 'I'm sure I don't know *what* to call you!'

'You may go now, Corse.'

'I will see that she does not stir from this room!' said Osorio upon this to the discouraged Corse, with cowboy-jaw to the fore to back up his assurance.

'Will you, sir? I'm afraid she won't take much notice of you, Mr Potter.'

'Yes, I will guarantee that she does not leave this room!'

'It would take more than you to stop me!' Baby remarked, without looking up from *Lady Chatterley's Lover*.

Osorio Potter produced from his hip pocket a large automatic pistol. It was his gat. He tapped it with his other hand, as he held it in his palm.

'You can go away with an easy mind, Miss Corse,' he said, patting it several times. 'I will attend to the prisoner!'

'Whatever are you doing with *that*!' exclaimed Miss Corse, pointing to the pistol.

'When I say a thing I mean it!' said Osorio, with the terrible terseness of the Bad Man on screens or in books.

'Oh, do put that thing away, Osorio!' Donald said. 'We all know you're a tough guy, but I'm sick of seeing the beastly thing! I'm positive it will go off one of these days!'

'One of these days it *will*!' Osorio said with great grimness. And he gazed very steadily indeed at the back of Donald Butterboy as he said it, his teeth set.

'Oh dear!' said Miss Corse. 'I suppose I shall have to stop here now.'

'Not at all!' said Osorio. 'The contrary.'

'It's your fault if you do,' said Baby reading her book. 'I've told you we require you no more for the present, Corse.'

'Oh, dear me!' said Corse, and sat down. 'You're not half a fair handful, the lot of you!'

CHAPTER 12

DINNER was not far off. The emergency kitchen staff was functioning at maximum pressure – in a veritable Turkish bath, below sea-level, in a culinary crypt difficult to ventilate – as likewise the robotic squads of clean-limbed men-servants, at their full war-complement, with overplus, liveried and unliveried (at whom Miss Bucktrout did by no means omit to make a thousand sheep's-eyes) as they marched and countermarched, in the atriums, fumoriums, lectoriums, ambulatories and lavatories, and the vast clangorous apartments – as if built to accommodate a tattoo, or, for size, of such proportions as to satisfy a metropolitan garrison in the matter of a parade-ground – of Beverley Chase, which had been constructed by a millionaire imitator of Strawberry Hill. It was the climax of the day – both for underdog and overdog. All stomachs stood still, in the bodies of the latter, and growled '*For what we are about to receive may the Lord make us truly thankful!*' And the Lord, although Beverley Chase was not the only place He had to attend to at this hour, *did* spare a moment to do as He was asked and deal with this important grace, and *did* inspire with a sort of *Thank you!* spirit the entire company. But it was, of course, only at dinner that this could come out as it should. It was a question of '*about* to receive' for a hectic half-hour yet.

But in the private suite of the hostess, or however we should call the large flat where she lived, in the centre of her own labyrinth, Mrs Wellesley-Crook lay at full length on one settee, in statuesque relaxation, but palpably dead-beat, and Donald Butterboy upon the other – all in, it was but too patent as well. Donald was curled up, actually, in a picturesque coil expressive of the *in extremis* condition of a waterless plant – the closing-in upon itself of an exhausted leaf (probably of a lily, almost certainly so, in fact). A doctor would have snapped the one word *Aspirin* a mile off. *Headache* was written all over both, in block-capitals, of giant Advert-script.

'Mercy!' gasped the lady of the house, breaking a tenminute silence (by her watch): 'I shall be just *thankful* and leave it at that, when all this *horde*' (she pronounced it like *hard* but the guttural *r* was the word really, one of at least twenty letters, *r* beside *r* beside *r* – with an aspirate to start it off and a feeble *d* to bring it to an end) 'when this lousy *horde* moves on!'

'How I do agree with you, Maisie!' Donald weakly but warmly acquiesced.

'They are the most untidy and dirty – yes, Donald, positively *non-clean* – set of people that it has ever been my *lot* . . . !'

'Or mine! However, they'll break camp on Monday morning.'

'Break camp! That just expresses what I feel my house has been made into! The place is nothing but a *canteen*!'

'I know – it makes me quite queasy. Half of them are disgustingly drunk. I saw one being sick just now in the passage.'

'The servants say they can do nothing with them.'

'I pity the servants from the bottom of my heart.'

'One man locks his toothbrush up in his suitcase after he has used it. There is a woman who stopped Mrs Kemp and asked her if she could wash a nightdress. 'No, madam,' she said when she saw it, 'I will burn it for you if you like!'

'How feeel-thy, Maisie, please don't tell me any more!'

'The East Wing is like the steerage of an emigrant ship. Have you seen it, Donald?'

'Have I not, could I help it? – I went there to see Potter just now.'

'The servants call it the Third Class – I wouldn't go near it if my life depended on it – I should *slap* somebody, I know.'

'I'm positive you would. The bedrooms are like beargardens – I couldn't help seeing two or three as I passed.'

'Beargardens! A bear is a gentleman compared with . . . !'

'True. And the passages are full of Black-Hand plots.'

'I shouldn't wonder at that.'

'The lavatory has become a urinal!' he screamed. 'All the plugs are broken. I believe the wives of some of them have brought their washing with them – I saw stockings on a hot-water pipe.'

'The women, my dear, are the worst. But you have to ask their women.'

'Oh, I know – you needn't tell me about it all, Maisie,' Donald slobbered, in despair, 'and it is all *my* fault Maisie, it is terrible!'

'Nonsense, Donald!'

'Yes it is – I told you not to do it, but you *would*!'

'Don't be such a silly boy, Donald – it doesn't matter to me a little bit really, I'm just not myself tonight – it's the price one has to pay for fame, that's how you must look at it.'

'I am beginning to feel, Maisie, more strongly every minute, that I was born to blush unseen.'

'Oh don't talk like that, Donald – *unseen*! When this is all over I shall go up to London for a week or two while this house is being fumigated, that's all. Forget it!'

'Oh I hate myself – what a *nuisance* I am to everybody!'

Mrs Wellesley-Crook got up and going over to him placed

an imperial hand upon his forehead, which was oddly enough so cool as to be rather pleasant – for *her* blood was really a little over normal, as if she needed a pill.

'You are feverish, Donald!' she said, gazing down at him with fierce solicitude, as if she would make a meal of him as soon as look at him, for her face was cast upon uncompromising lines – the Crooks were a pioneer stock, from the rugged gutters of Chicago, and their faces showed it. 'Don't worry any more and be a silly boy!'

'I can't *help* it,' wailed the Book-of-the-Week-Prize-winner-to-be.

Mrs Wellesley-Crook, at a sign from a maid who had entered meanwhile, passed into a neighbouring room, in which Donald could hear her telephoning energetically. In not many minutes she was back again. Her manner had undergone a decided change for the brisker and brighter – the professional hostess had put on her mental armour in the next room, or the next room but one. As she stalked in now it was like a piece of America moving, as if a determined fragment of the Rocky Mountains had got over into Oxfordshire by mistake.

'I think you have made some progress, Donald,' she told him, sinking into a chair and extending her hand to a table for a Lucky Strike packet, an English habit she had recently acquired. She was dressed like a barbarous queen, moved like one, and felt pretty well like one most of the time, but what state or century impossible to fix: regality – plainly at a barbaric stage of culture – so much one got; though a Jewess in Paris was responsible for the outfit in fact, down to the African manacles that rattled ironically upon her wrists. Donald looked at her out of one eye – for he had not moved at all – Maisie inspired him with uneasiness in the evening, as she was twice his size. He could not banish the thought that she might have some odd rite hidden in the darker depths of her American nature – after night-fall he was generally a little on his guard with her.

'I believe everything will come all right, anyway,' she said, with a massive sigh.

'What is that, Maisie?' he lisped, with dozing lips, a little painted.

'It seems to me that you have made some headway, Donald.'

'What is that, Maisie?'

'Headway, Donald.'

'Oh.'

'I have spoken privately to two or three of these people. There is that man who gives the Sévigné-Stavisky prize. He spoke very highly of your book indeed!'

'He hasn't seen it, Maisie – what are you talking about!'

'No, but he will pass up *the prize*, Donald, which is the main thing after all – you mustn't expect too much of them.'

'Unless they *read* it, Maisie . . .'

'Oh, *read* it? Why yes, but don't *fuss* so, Donald – these are busy men. There's that fat man who is Scotch, I think, he spoke very *highly* of you indeed, Donald. I asked him if he thought you had any chance of the prize – what is his prize? I forget which, but it's one of them: he told me, *in the greatest confidence*, Donald, that you should have it if he had any say in the matter. And I understand he is the only man that has any say. So that is that. And that Literary Larceny affair, it seems that will undoubtedly be given you because they say you have – "cribbed" was their expression – it's an English expression – a book written four years ago by a girl who cut her throat, after getting the prize for the Worst Book of the Season – perhaps you remember, I don't, but it doesn't signify.'

Donald started up into a sitting position, haggard, his hands clasped upon the settee in front of him.

'Oh, that's a lie! Cribbed *what*? Who was it, Maisie, told you that disgusting lie? *I* know who it was – I can guess!'

'Never mind, it doesn't signify any.'

'But it *does*, don't you see! I shall be ruined! It was that horrid Mrs Hyman!'

'No, dear – it doesn't matter *at* all!'

'It *does*, don't you understand – the horrid old cat!'

'It doesn't, Donald – I happen to have inquired.'

'How do you mean?'

'Well I thought it might be prejudicial – that did occur to me.'

'Of course it is.'

'No, Donald – I saw Mr Shodbutt and talked the matter over with him. He said it was most unfair of Mrs Hyman and *quite untrue*.'

'Of course it is!'

'Well, he said she was doing it to annoy him, and he would – *stake his critical reputation* was what he said – that you had never seen the girl's book.'

'Nor have I – the old beast. Oh how I do hate her, don't you, Maisie? Why, the girl's book was called *It Takes* Three *to Make a Bedroom-Scene!* The difference in title alone proves the lie up to the hilt!'

'He said it was the same plot – and *subject*, oh yes, and *style*, he said, and that some of the passages were word for word like yours, but he would point out in his article, he said, that such things were common among real geniuses, who have second sight he says – now *listen*, Donald, since you're one of them! – and are so telepathic and televisional that it is *perfectly remarkable* he says they are ever able to write anything original *at* all!'

'Shoddie's a capital old fellow, what! – he's the best of the whole boiling of them!' almost shouted the rapturous Donald at this – whose headache had departed as if by black magic and who was sitting up *and* taking a great deal of notice indeed for a lazy boy as he was — clasping and unclasping the restless tentacles of his hands. 'Bravo *Shottboot*, as good old Taxi calls him — I hope you thanked him; I will though.'

'You'll do nothing of the sort! All this is *most* confidential.'

'Is it a secret, Maisie?'

'Of course, silly boy!'

She stroked his haggardly hanging hair — she had got up to move about as she had become restless — her lips pursed into a smile of alarming maternity and her eagle eyes dreaming on the ceiling, what about, it was impossible to conjecture, except what is proper to a bird of prey, in a tender moment.

'Don't, Maisie, you're hurting!' Donald said.

She withdrew her hand slowly with a rapt smile and patted her own carefully disciplined headgear, looking towards a glass.

'You must run away and dress, Donald darling,' she said. 'Oh, and Donald, there is one thing I forgot to mention, it's about that dark boy.'

'Who's that?'

She fixed her spreadeagle eyes with their full senatorial American severity upon him, and uttered the one syllable:

'*Podd'r!*'

'What's that — what?' he asked.

'Oss-sorr-ree-oh!'

'Oh, Osorio you mean — what about him?'

'Well. That boy, Mr Shodbutt told me, came up to him and said you were his best man.'

'No. He must have said that he was mine. But he's batty. Take no notice of him!'

'It doesn't signify — he was yours then, or you were his.'

'All the same.'

'But he was *very rude* to Mr Shodbutt, Donald!'

'Rude, Maisie? How awful. He can't be anything else, you know – he's always rude, it means nothing.'

'Yes, very rude. He handed Mr Shodbutt a manuscript, it seems. He handed it to Mr Shodbutt and said, "Here, Shodbutt, old boy – take this upstairs and read it. Tell me what you think of it at once. I give you till eleven tonight!" That's what he said. Then he left Mr Shodbutt with this great wad of chapters – for it was a story it seems – in his hand. Mrs Shodbutt said as he went away he laughed and said, "Mind, *eleven*. I shall wait no longer!" What do you think of that, Donald? He's a dangerous boy, isn't he?'

'What did Shodbutt make of the book, did he say?'

'I asked him that, yes. He said it was the greatest – now let me see – the "biggest *tripe* . . ."?'

'Tripe – yes, that's right. *Tripe!* Oh, Osorio – poor darling! he will be enraged: how lovely – *tripe!*'

'Mr Shodbutt said he would tell him so.'

A gong boomed.

'Donald, darling, you must *hurry!*'

Donald rose and swayed where he stood, passing his hand over his temples without touching them, like the pseudo-asiatics of the snake-dance of the British Stage, for he was extremely British of course, in a derogatory sense, though he might not see eye-to-eye with Sweet Alice Benbolt.

'What fun, Maisie, Osorio will probably shoot Shodbutt – he is armed to the teeth!'

'I'll watch he doesn't do anything of the sort.'

'How fearfully funny!' Donald appeared to be really somewhat tickled at his best man's discomfiture, in a dreamy and dreary snake-dancing fashion of his own, which almost suggested that the Book of the Week business did not leave him quite so cold as all that, even at this time of day. 'He's always so superior about prizes too. My poor Osorio – you will never get it now!' Donald indulged in a mock lament, and laughed artificially, showing his gums.

'Get it! What do you mean – Shodbutt's prize? Of course he won't, you may depend on that! Besides, it's not printed.'

'No, but I mean *never*. He insisted upon coming here, to bully Shodbutt into giving it him next year, or when it comes out.'

'Do you believe that's so?'

'Osorio's very ambitious.'

Kissing the tips of his fairy fingers at Maisie, Donald fled – a sylph-like tornado, dragging off his jacket from one shoulder only as he went.

CHAPTER 13

THE dinner was somewhat wilder than the lunch. Excited by the rainbow cocktails to a great nervous pitch, several of the guests showed all their colours immediately, under the influence of the torrents of champagne, lavished by the hostess to elicit any prize-giving propensity present in any one of these politely lettered guests; and to seal the pact between her and this bunch of the oddest of bread-winners — that *her* god should be *their* god, and that all their prizes should be his prizes — for was he not a Butterboy among Butterboys! And her fierce prairie-sweepers of eyes, with the extremity of maudlin motherhood, were madly alight, as, with a majestic roguishness, she lifted her glass, first to this, and then to that, prize-giver — as though to say, 'Well! Here's how. Here's to *our* Donald Butterboy — the cutest little Britisher that ever trod the High!' And they returned the toast in foaming goblets, nothing loath, fixing her with a knowing opposite eye, as if to say 'Trust me! The prize is his as sure as your name's Crook!'

All hearts were warmed towards the family of the Crooks — there was no flaw in the harmonious concert of cordial good relations as between host and guest (whatever private reservations this or that prize-giver might entertain regarding Butterboy, though certainly most of such decided to give him their prizes and so set the seal on his genius). But if this was the case as between guest and host, it was by no means the same as between guest and guest. And, as the wine did its work, some rampant animosities declared themselves in a quiet way withal and that in quarters where at other times a certain degree of discipline prevailed – upon a basis of honour amongst racketeers, and upon the principle of *foul play's a jewel*.

If it were at all possible to plot this complex panorama of personalities it would be safe to say that the main line of cleavage was to be looked for between those who made a hearty living by the well-puffed pen (or by the pen that did the best-seller puffing in the biggest Press) on the one hand, and those whose well-puffed pens were puffed differently, upon the other – not puffed for *gain* but for sheer *pride of place*; who sought not even to best-sell, because, being comfortably circumstanced, the commercial lure was less, and pride of place was all in all. These latter were the 'highbrows' of course – *they* were just *geniuses* pure and simple – rather than geniuses *in spite of* such inflated popular publics as precluded their books being anything but of a consummate badness and poorness that it was really impossible to disguise (where their highbrow partners in iniquity pretended to great things and were monuments – but private monuments – of impeccable taste). And however much the merely best-selling geniuses pointed to the great journeyman penman Daniel Defoe, it was easy enough for their highbrow antagonists to point out that, apart from the fact that these best-sellers had very few *Crusoes* or *Journals of the Plague* to their credit, anyway, the times were strikingly different and no such comparison held water – not as between conditions so dissimilar, of publicity, politics, and the rest. Books mass-produced with us and artificially made 'famous' in quick succession, by a tremendously highly-organized *Puffing-machine* as it were (for each and all of these puffers were quite ready to discourse about puffing at any moment – their attitude was that *they had nothing to hide*, which was true enough since it would be impossible to hide it, it 'jumped to the eye') – the careers of books mass-produced could not be compared with the careers of books, and their authors, in the days of Defoe. The best-sellers, however, didn't mind much, they had their answer: for *they* could do some pointing-out as well! namely that the jolly old 'highbrow'-racket, for all their beastly superiority, did not grow brows *quite* as high as Milton or as Swift and that a miss is as good as a mile. For if one could not be Defoe (the standard example of the mere journalist-of-genius) why then by Jove and by Jesus the *other* fellow shouldn't get away with the laurels of the intellectual sage either! And anyway, what books had these donnish scoffers to their credit (for it was a mistake to suppose that *writing about* Milton and Swift made you into a Milton or a Swift – an error of the donnish mind, the best-sellers objected)? Yes, as to their *books* (growled the militant best-sellers), they were those of Mrs Hyman! – which, as Mrs Hyman's partisans very well knew (since whether we *puff to sell* to the Many, or whether we *puff to impress* the Few, we are all puffers together nevertheless, are we not?) had been *puffed* into the inflated position they held! And so the guerrilla warfare took its sleepy course – that of the High, the Middle, and the Low Brow; neither side was strong enough to hurt the other very much, or cared enough about it perhaps to do so, if they could – it was just a bitter little bicker, nothing more, and nobody minded a great deal. Really it was a sort of *alliance* – the terms of which left to the one party all the *swank*, to the other party all the *swag*!

But Shodbutt now – *he* was different! He was very conceited! He claimed in a sense both the *swank* and the *swag*! He wanted both the best-selling sheckles *and* the pride of place. He was an awkward customer!

Now Shodbutt was certainly no gentleman and certainly had by legacy got no gold except only by the sweat of his brow; and certainly Shodbutt was, in consequence, upon the journeyman, upon the *professional* side of the racket. Shodbutt was the 'Player' distinctly, rather than the 'Gentleman'. And very touchy at that about his status, very touchy indeed!

Yes, Shodbutt, probably because of his inordinate vanity, was a man who minded more than most. And he imported a good healthy tincture of venom into his exchanges with the Hyman faction and all of the donnish ilk. He fought the age-old *snobbish* division in the game of Letters in Great Britain, and he fought it tooth and nail; he did not care, he *would* not emerge upon the field, as it were, at Lord's, at the Players' entrance: no, he *would* come out to bat side by side with the so-called Gentlemen, at the place where *they* came out or not at all. The Score Board (that is to say the *Sales Index*) was all that signified in this matter. He knocked up a tidy bit every time that he batted, did he not? – and, well, as *umpire* he was in a class by himself! (And there he drew the class-line very firmly indeed, where *he* was the class!) Well then – to hell with all these highbrow airs and *especially* with those of Mrs Rhoda Hyman, who had appointed herself his *bête noire* in perpetuity!

The only difficulty was, and it was a major one, that Mrs Hyman was *a woman*. This was an obstacle to a gloves-off set-to. For Shodbutt was nothing if not the Gentleman (in spite of his scorn of the snobbish and all its works) and a Gentleman never hits a lady below the belt, does he? – but what am I saying – is it permissible that he should hit her *at all*? Shodbutt thought not. So an exquisite frustration was set up within Shodbutt and his relationship *vis-à-vis* Mrs Hyman was one of the most troublesome problems of a long life. Panoplied in the woman's privilege – and subtly armed with the defensive and offensive equipment of *the lady* as well – she sat there and looked slyly at him. There were times when he nearly burst his starch-stiff front to get at her and have it out as man to man. Tonight was one of those occasions. He looked at her very hard indeed and he could not help himself when he remarked, catching her watery eye:

'I'm glad to hear, Mrs Hyman, that all adages are not fallacious.'

'What do you mean by that, Mr Shodbutt?' she politely inquired.

'I was thinking of the saying — *Set a thief to catch a thief.*'

Mrs Hyman smiled so faintly that the lightest summer breeze would have blown the smile off her face and left only the weary-willy mask of a great authoress, bowed down with the stupidity of Man.

'You admit then it is a catch?' she said. 'Do you?'

'No I don't!' blurted Shodbutt gloomily at her. 'I admit nothing!'

'I'm afraid I don't understand you then.'

And Rhoda Hyman, with a parting look of weary abstraction at him, bang in his face, just for a second or two, turned away to talk to her French neighbour.

Mrs S.S. signalled (it was an inverted S.O.S.) to S.S. from her distant seat. But Samuel merely shrugged his shoulders crossly — he was put out, he refused to enter into communication with any of Mrs Hyman's sex, even Mrs Samuel Shodbutt.

Sir Titus said to Osorio:

'Why so pensive, Osorio?'

And Osorio replied, his eyes smouldering with ill-ventilated passion:

'I am thinking out a *plot* for a *crime*!'

'Not, I hope, a real crime, Osorio?'

'Yes, a real one. I'm sick of counterfeit articles!'

Sir Titus bent over towards him.

'I wish you'd put that man out of the way for me!'

'Which?'

'That one.'

Sir Titus indicated a little man with half a moustache and large blue peepers, who was sucking up to Miss Stella Salt, very successfully too.

Mrs Wellesley-Crook remarked to Butterboy, in a low voice:

'Donald, that dark boy has not looked in Mr Shodbutt's direction once so far – he means mischief, it seems to me.'

'Mischief?' croaked the somewhat tipsy Butterboy. 'What next – he's my best man!'

At this moment Osorio could be observed indicating Shodbutt with his finger to Sir Titus, and Butterboy exclaimed:

'It's all right, Maisie – he's pointing at Mr Shodbutt now!'

'So I see,' said Mrs Crook. 'I don't like it at all – he's not a nice boy, I'm afraid.'

'Not a nice boy! What do you mean, Maisie? Still, have it as you like!'

Taking his name-card from beside his plate, Donald Butterboy scribbled upon it a line or two, and handing it to a passing footman said 'Give this to Mr Potter, please – twenty seats down, across the road: that dark young gentleman talking to the dirty old man in an eyeglass'.

Osorio received the card upon which Donald had scribbled the note, and he read as follows, his brows knitted, savaging his lips with cruel white teeth:

It's no use your looking at Sam Shod, he's turned down your book. He's told Maisie it's rotten. Condoléances. Donald.

Miss Stella Salt was observing to her neighbour:

'Uncle Shodbutt has been asked here to give that young man his prize. And you'll see he'll do it.'

'Do you think he will.'

'Of course, he is gaga.'

'What, S.S.?'

'Yes — and suffers from a bad swelled head, which is dangerous at his time of life.'

Monsieur Jolat was roaring at Rhoda Hyman:

'Mais parfaitement! C'était formidable! C'est inouie!'

'Oui?' answered Mrs Hyman, shrinking away from the big vociferous Burgundian — for to *read* was in a way more suitable than to *hear* it. This particular vessel was almost too much alive and kicking. Yes, he was much too much alive! And a pint or two perhaps of the fermented liquor for which the French soil was so famous had found its way down his throat. Burgundy and champagne did *not* improve the taste of the French tongue for a really sensitive ear, about that there was no question — and for a literary mind the stony labyrinth of the ear was as much more mighty than the palate, as the pen was mightier than the sword. Racine in-the-flesh — *Racine drunk*, if such a thing could be admitted within the pale of possibility — would be a very different matter to a page of *Bérénice*.

Richard Dritter winked, from the distance, at Sir Titus L'Estrange, and Sir Titus waved his hand — out of the far-away and long-ago of the days of *Under the Hill*.

Monsieur Jolat wiped his beard and vociferated again, *à tue-tête*:

'C'est formidable! C'est à s'y méprendre!'

Rhoda Hyman, who had a weakness for beards, notwithstanding felt a little sick and looked over at Shodbutt. Shodbutt was picking a tooth with his tongue, and, as her eye encountered his, tongue, cheek and tooth had just realized that smart percussion like the noise of a kiss, by means of which the commercial traveller makes himself known to other gentlemen on the road. Shodbutt felt a little damp under the collar, for he believed that Mrs Hyman had been brought to look over at him by the distinctive sound of the low-bred tooth-tricks, that her staring eyes wanted to know 'What's that?'

Osorio was sombre. Sir Titus leaned towards him and insinuated, very archly indeed:

'It takes *two* to make a bedroom-scene!'

'It depends what sort of bedroom-scene you mean,' Osorio answered darkly. 'But *two* is a good number!'

'A *beautiful* number!'

Osorio shrugged his shoulders contemptuously.

'Two is company!' whispered Sir Titus hoarsely.

'Too much company sometimes,' Osorio Potter said. 'One from one leaves *none*!'

Baby Bucktrout, who sat opposite Osorio, was not on speaking terms with him at present.

'You see that young man over there?' she said to her left-hand neighbour, who was the big noise on the board of the Biennial Special Award for the Best Homicide, who nodded. 'He's fond of gardeners.'

'Indeed? He looks as though he might be a flower-lover.'

'He's a very, interfering young man. He ought not to be here at all.'

'There are many people here whom I am rather surprised to find in such a place.'

'Yes. But they're all here because of old Donald's book.'

'What book is that?' asked the big noise with affected innocence.

'Haven't you heard? *It Takes Two to Make a Bedroom-Scene!*'

'Oh. A very promising title!'

'He cribbed it, though, from an American book.'

The chairman of the B.S.A.B.H., who was an Irishman, lifted his eyebrows.

'That is interesting – he is evidently a young man of resource.'

'You'd better not be funny about him – he is my future husband.'

'Indeed!'

'And that's his best man.'

'What, the young man who is an authority on rock-gardens?'

'Yes. So he says – but if I were marrying Donald – not that I am – I'd refuse to have him. He is sly.'

'I see. You'd put your veto on him.'

'For form's sake. One must do the thing properly if one does it at all.'

Joanie's neighbour, one of the two gentlemen who had witnessed the accolade bestowed by the coal-black mammie upon Taxi, asked:

'What is that young man's name, did you say, who is sitting next to Mrs Wellesley-Crook?'

'Butterboy. Donald Butterboy.'

'Is he related to Sir Boswell Butterboy?'

'He is his son, I believe.'

'They call it *Butterby*.'

'Do they? Yes, I believe I've heard that they do.'

There seemed to be hundreds and hundreds of guests though there may not have been so many, people are difficult to count: in the course of the afternoon a number of late arrivals had made their appearance with many apologies, and there were overflow tables in this gargantuan refectory of the lavish Crooks. These were reserved for the performers, particularly – for those who *wrote* the stuff, that is to say, in contradistinction to those who sold it or those who selected, priced or puffed it: for of course by work, of however inferior a nature, no man may hope to make as much money as the one who handles and markets the labour of others; and as to power, that *alter ego* of money, clearly no individual – whether he be a fine or a common one – can possess as much if he be one who merely produces, as he who trafficks in, or sets up as an expert about, what is produced by other men. It is the female function to produce, and with that goes the female handicap.

So to this discriminatory dinner-table arrangement nobody could possibly take exception, since a fundamental social law, of unchallengeable standing, was involved; and since such writers of books as had been asked were only second-best-sellers, or only a few of those in the first class had responded (such functions as these acquiring gradually a lowbrow air for some of the real élite, once firmly in the saddle – the world of books having its Greta Garbos, with their 'great artist' airs, as much as the sister-world of mass-produced film sob-stuff and kiss-stuff, or gunman-romance). In the nature of things this was, as far as possible, a commercial gathering *pur sang*, of representative people belonging to a booming 'young' industry – financiers and contractors, agents and touts, middlemen of every description, *and* a few characteristic specimens of the better-paid pen-pushing wage-slaves of same. And Mrs Rhoda Hyman was there as the ambassador of the Intellect, so to speak, but was in the business herself as well, so all was ship-shape and properly true to type.

Among this handful of odd handiworkers, however, named in derision 'authors', there was none odder than old Mrs Boniface, who had just entered upon her eighty-seventh summer, and whose first novel had been published but a fortnight before, receiving the much-coveted award of the Best First Novel of the Year – for which a thousand 'authors' and a good lashing of greedy publishers had struggled tooth and nail, pulling every wire upon which there was a handsbreadth left for anyone to lay hold of. But old Mrs Boniface got it. And Shodbutt had said, in his weekly Monday blurb in the *Outcry* that if he had not already made his decision regarding the Book of the Week Prize and given it to nineteen-year-old Daisy Swivell (for her *Solway Dane*) and if that book had not been the greatest novel in the language – except perhaps the translation of *The Idiot* (and he was prepared to stake his critical reputation upon that statement) – he would not have hesitated a moment to bestow his critical accolade – with as much critical gusto as forty years' experience had imbued a critic with, whose enthusiasm had augmented daily, or he should perhaps have said *weekly*, instead of becoming tempered with a lily-livered caution (as was the case, he was sorry to say, with *some* of his more pretentious colleagues) – he should not have held back a second from conferring it upon the immortal pages of *Footsteps in the Sand* – which literally smelt of the Seventies in the way that Cologne smelt of its Eau, or Naples of its garlic.

Mrs Boniface took rank with the big prize-givers and was within shouting distance of the hostess, who shouted to her quite a lot, calling upon her to clear up this or that point, and once winking at her in a burst of unrestrainable broadminded *bonhomie*. Into everyone's face who happened to glance in her direction a far-away-and-long-ago look 'stole' (the stealth was but too painfully apparent) – a sickly smiling of the eyes took place, along with such a smiling faintness, or such a faint smiling, of the lips, as suggested that ever so little more of *that* smile and a big sob would just wreck the whole social mask altogether, and she or he who owned it would have to leave the table for the rest of the meal.

Everybody in his immediate neighbourhood vied with everyone else to help her to salt (regardless of proverbial sorrow ensuing – of which she must have experienced so much anyway as to make an extra pinch of it of very little consequence), picked up her lace handkerchief when she dropped it from her trembling hands, read the menu for her, translating the French, shouted in her ear or tried to catch her eye and throw her a lovely kind-hearted grimace. A nursing-home atmosphere was in fact created in that part of the dinner-table. As liveried footmen approached the place where Mrs Boniface sat they became conscious of passing over into a description of doldrums – a soothing and welcome *hush* contrasting sharply with all around it. It was *The Land of Undertones* (to make use of the title of a book by the lady who sat next but one to this latest type of literary gold-mine).

'Did you ever write anything before?' inquired her neighbour, the editor of *Feature and Fiction*.

'Never!' piped Mrs Boniface. 'Never. I wanted to but my husbands wouldn't let me!' And she wagged her old waxen head with a roguish demureness and peeped out of the pits of her eyes at the gallant editor.

('That old girl would have made her fortune in Hollywood!' whispered one of them in the charmed circle to the lady next to him. 'Yes,' said the young lady, 'but she is not doing so badly with her pen.' 'I know,' said he, 'but she can't get all that across with a fountain pen.' And the young lady observer of the old bookworld lion, or lioness, in question, agreed.)

'Were you married more than once? I didn't know,' startled at the plural she had employed, the editor remarked.

'Oh yes. First I was Mrs Fisher, for four halcyon years.' Her eyes watered, it was the tabasco on the oysters, and the editor turned his head away: 'Next Mrs Mintzer, after that I was Mrs Mackay-Arbucle – a strict man, Scotch you know, but a Godfearing one, he was a corn chandler – then Mrs Hawkwood; Mrs Boyne next – Mr Boyne was a vet, a very

Godfearing man and a great dog-lover, may God rest his soul. Last, Mrs Boniface, as I am now.'

'Last but not *least*!' her neighbour neighed heartily. 'Last but not least, Mrs Boniface!'

'Well, that maybe, who can tell,' she replied, 'who can tell. I sometimes wish that it had been as Mrs Mintzer that I had written my first book.'

'Why is that? Was Mr Mintzer . . . ?'

'Poor Mr Mintzer was in the undertaking business – it was a terrible shock when he was taken off himself. I feel he would have liked seeing his name in the papers, however it got there – and he did set his face it is quite true against my writing down my thoughts as I sometimes did. He would have been the man to understand what it meant to be *immortal* – as Mr Shodbutt put it – would Mr Mintzer, of that I am positive. His calling, you see, would have come in there to help him to see that.'

'Yes, one can see how it might do that – I can see that, Mrs Boniface.'

'He had his heart and soul in his business. Immortality, that would have meant a great deal to poor dear Mr Mintzer. It would have meant more than all the rest to Mr Mintzer.'

'But are you not thrilled yourself, Mrs Boniface, at the thought that you are to be immortal?' asked the editor of *Feature and Fiction* kindly, preparing to make a mental note of the reply.

'Well, I must own that at first – I am a poor weak vessel – I felt it was very nice. But I feel it is taking advantage, if you understand me.'

The editor, baffled for a moment, frowned.

'Taking advantage, Mrs Boniface? Stealing a march, perhaps upon *Time*, eh? Is that the idea?'

'No,' the old lady replied. 'I'm thinking of my dear lamented Henry.'

This was evidently the undertaker, the central figure in *Footsteps in the Sands*. Mrs Boniface wiped a few drops of convenient water away from her left eye, which had been more particularly affected by the tabasco. The editor of *Feature and Fiction* respected the dear old lady's emotion, and returned to his Whitstables until this flood of bitter memory should have subsided.

But there was another heroine of the hour who would have run Mrs Boniface pretty close, if the gold rush in her case were not almost over – for her first novel had been out seven weeks – and that was little Nancy Cozens, aged eleven and a half. *Bursting Ripe* had sold twenty-five thousand on the day of publication, it had been triumphantly announced, and the public had swallowed two more 'large impressions'. As a veteran of eighteen she would doubtless look back upon this day as the culmination of her career – although she was far lower down the table than she would have been only three weeks ago. This table was like a graph in its distribution of the name-cards, and Nancy's curve was a sharply descending one. She was still glamorous with the best-selling boastfulness of her publishers, nevertheless; but they *had* released six other glamorous names since hers. That was the situation.

At present, however, she showed no signs of *looking back*. Her eyes were as sparkling with fun and pure cussedness as you could find in the eyes of any little lady of eleven and a half with all her life before her – instead of one who was a world-famous authoress, upon the crest of the wave (even if upon the wrong side of the crest as it happened, since there is no such thing commercially as 'a second novel' – there is only a 'first novel' and after that the deluge more or less). Two hemispheres had been thrilled by Nancy, she having received the American Book of the Month Club's cheque (which is guaranteed to sell eighty thousand copies before publication, or was when Nancy lived) but likewise that of the Novel League of Great Britain. It was some *dot* for a little lady of eleven! Shodbutt had expressed himself a staggered – 'I am an old hand,' he had written. 'I am wary! It takes a good deal to shake me out of my rut. But *Bursting Ripe* left me speechless – it uprooted me – I didn't know when I put it down whether I was standing on my head or my heels. I can say no more. All I *will* say is – READ IT! Do not read it once – read it twenty times: and if the first copy wears out (as mine did) order a second from your bookseller. I say advisedly, *order from your bookseller*, for this is not a book to borrow, merely, from a library: it is a book to *buy* and *keep*, as long as you have breath in your body, as I shall do. It shall never leave my shelves. I would rather part with all Jane Austen at one fell swoop – and that for me is saying a mouthful, for I yield to no one in doglike faithfulness to our premier lady novelist. I take my hat off to her every time. But I take off my hat to Nancy Cozens even more. I loudly affirm that I never put the damn thing on at all! I remain bareheaded, as one does in the presence of the ultimate things, such as death. But this is *birth*. I remain uncovered! It is pure *creation*!'

Her neighbour, the husband of Mrs Wheelwright, one of the five big noises on the Novel League committee, and a quiet but respected workman in the bookselling factory, who clocked in every morning at eight (as of course social life began at twelve-thirty with its sherries and gin fizzes) but who would not have been so near the centre of the table if it had not been for his wife, said to little Nancy:

'Are you busy with a second book, I expect you are?'

'No,' she said, a slight cloud passing over the young landscape of her expressive face. 'I'm busy training for the table-tennis championship just now and I feel to write a book would cramp my style.'

'Do you suffer from writer's cramp perhaps?'

'Oh no. I mean it would take the edge off my training – anything sedentary – I must sit down to write, though I know a lot of girls who don't.'

'Of course. Do you know a lot of girl novelists?'

'Let me see. I know about six or seven. But they're not good. Their plots are childish.'

'Yes, the plot's the thing. You have a plot!'

'Mrs Wheelwright said that I had style.'

'Yes, but you have plot. Do you map out your plot in detail before you sit down to write?'

'Oh no, the plot comes to me as I go along. It isn't a plot really. When it's finished it's a plot.'

'Yes, of course.'

But upon the other side of little Miss Nancy Cozens was no less a person than Osorio Potter – no *less* a person from our point of view, perhaps, but the fact that Nancy was next to a guest of the calibre of Osorio showed how far she had fallen from the rank that, as the author of *Bursting Ripe*, twenty-four hours after publication she would unquestionably have occupied.

At the word *plot* (overheard as Mr Wheelwright had insisted *You have a plot!*) Potter picked up his ears. And now, as Nancy turned her attention once more to the food that no wholehearted table-tennis champion would have tolerated on her plate, he remarked:

'The plot doesn't matter a straw!'

'Don't you think so?' Nancy looked under her lashes sideways at the big masterful boy.

'Only in real life,' he said.

'How do you mean? How can you have a plot in real life?'

'I mean in a book the plot's not the thing, it can have too much plot.'

'Oh yes. Far too much.'

'It's only in real life the plot matters.'

'But what sort of plots?'

'Well, the Gunpowder Plot was a plot. This is a plot too!'

And he waved his hand round the table, where certainly a fair amount of plotting was in progress, but Nancy, glancing about her, could not see how *that* 'had plot': so she squealed instead:

'Oh I do adore Guy Fawkes Day, don't you?'

She felt drawn to this funny boy who frowned so much.

'I can't say I do,' said Osorio.

'Those fireworks are so lovely that go off like bombs!'

'Um – yes.'

'It's just like what an air-raid must have been – Bang – crash! Boom-bang! I adore it!'

But Osorio's attention was unfortunately diverted by the mention of crackers: his mind turned to a conversation he had held with old Charlie in which crackers had played a prominent part. It was before he had finally realized quite how disturbingly 'different' old Charlie was. He had put down what he had then said to the fact that he was after all a sort of cop – and hence inclined to frown upon little lads who let off bursting crackers, to celebrate an unsuccessful political plot, but still a plot (although unsuccessful and political) against the government of the day – Old Charlie had cryptically inquired of him if he could tell him or not why it was that these guys (he had used guy in its American sense) were allowed to manufacture high explosive bomb-like fireworks which could shake a house and imitate the sounds of aerial-bombardments. As of course Osorio had not the remotest idea what that could signify, except a saturnalia for guttersnipes, and was sulkily mute, old Charlie had informed him that this alarming phenomenon derived from the same secret policy (consciously or not formulated and pursued) of the Old Gang – which referred, as all Charlie's jargon apparently did, not to romantic underworld gangs of 'killers' but to the dull old gentlemen who composed those boring political entities known as Cabinets: and Charlie identified the 'policy' (a word that always reminded Osorio of the word 'police') that countenanced the manufacture of needlessly powerful squibs with the policy that countenanced the flood of books and magazines keeping violent death well to the fore in the consciousness of all and sundry, and that condoned every crime of blood and hate provided it was make-believe – as though what was make-believe today was not grim earnest tomorrow, and if *games* of war or of crime did not promote the reality they simulated! 'This is the blood-psychosis,' Charlie had told him. 'What we are talking about is one manifestation only, however disguised, of the theory of "creative hatred". You are acquainted with that theory? It does not matter. It is the outcome of the Commune. *Haine créatrice* – what does that signify but that destruction is creation? You give birth in killing – the philosophy of the Evolutionary struggle, where *all* is battle and death, and the "birth" (the "creation") is a pious hope, no more. This annual bombardment of fireworks of heavier and heavier calibre, shattering the eardrums of the peaceful citizen, is a symptom of what we should all realize lies in wait for us just under the surface. The War never really ended; all this sort of thing is encouraged to keep the war-hysteria simmering, lest it should be too great a shock when they *do it again* – when the next mass-massacre is decided upon. For our rulers, for all their Conferences and Pacts, have never abandoned the idea of keeping up their sleeves another gigantic blood-letting, if their policies appear to demand it. They are mad automatons, they cannot adapt themselves to new circumstances. This is even what their Peace Conferences mean: for what good can come of a dozen nations wrangling incessantly as to how many bombing-planes or torpedoes this or that nation shall possess? It is as if we two were arguing how much arsenic each should possess for killing the other – *angrily* arguing too, backing up our reasons, for *the other*, having less, with terrible and cease-less threats.' What old Charlie was driving at was very far from plain, but like the interfering policeman that he was he resented (that was patent enough) the November night of loud explosions to which the firework-trade looked forward throughout the year. The more he thought of Charlie and the way he had been taken in by him, or taken him rather to be other than he was (just a cop through and through as he now recognized), the more he felt a certain uneasiness. Were other things as subject to progressive transformation or self-contradiction? Such was the kind of sensation he invariably encountered whenever he thought of Charlie. And Charlie had made a mystery of Guy Fawkes Day, of all things. Osorio would never be asked to 'Remember the old Guy!' now without some obscure, unboyish, reserve in his one-dimensional intellect, about the ritual of the bonfire of a simple conspirator, and its hypothetic relation to some im-pending disaster. Old Charlie had projected the shadow of the political policeman over the anniversary of a scarecrow in a steeple hat, surrounded by barrels of gunpowder on a par with Christmas stockings and Easter eggs. Sullenly brooding upon the shortcomings of Charlie he was almost startled to hear the voice of little Nancy chirp:

'I wish I could be in an air-raid. It is a great shame, I just missed the War.'

Osorio gazed at her a moment very hard, then he said with great abruptness:

'I hate the War. The thought of it bores me. A soldier for me is — well, just another sort of policeman.'

'But it must have been so *exciting* — for those not taking part of course.'

'If it's excitement you want, you should go to Chicago. That's the place.'

'I should love to go to Chicago. Have you been there?'

'No. But there are lots of Americans over here — *gunmen*!' he hissed fiercely in her ear.

'Are there? Where?'

'Everywhere. I talked to two last week. It was up in London. Their armpits were stiff with point-four-five automatics.'

'What, revolvers?'

'Yep!' answered Osorio, transatlantic for the occasion, rolling his eyes at her, and she rolling her eyes a little back at him.

'What fun! Weren't you pleased? I should have loved to be with you! Didn't you feel terribly bucked?'

'I? Oh, why should I be? They said they were Public Enemies.'

'How splendid.'

'But I didn't swallow that dope.'

'But were they "killers"? Were they real killers!'

'Yes. But just the usual kind.'

'Oh. But still!'

They both sat for a while, eating hungrily and gulping down their Mumm, Nancy thinking up further subjects in common and what next to say — since this big funny boy was on the strong silent side and it was no use pressing him to tell her more about the 'killers' he met: and Osorio broodily wondering what this kid was doing there, but supposing she must be with her people.

'Do you know all this crowd?' he asked her at last with a

lofty indifference, lifting his chin to be 'over the head of the crowd'.

'Oh now, I've only just come an hour ago.'

'Are you alone?'

'Yes. Are you?'

'Do you see that old fool down there – next to Mrs Wellesley-Crook?' he asked with a peculiar intentness, using his finger to point.

'Who? The grey-headed man with the small straggly moustache?'

'Yes. That's Shodbutt, the critic.'

A slight start and a perceptible contraction of the little brows betrayed an emotion in the breast of the little Nancy; not an agreeable one, it would seem. And this was understandable, in view of all the gasping and roaring on her account Shodbutt had done only six weeks ago, all the standing uncovered in the presence of birth as he might in the presence of death, and all the objurgations addressed to the public to go on buying fresh copies of *Bursting Ripe* as the old ones wore out – and seeing that not half an hour ago when her publisher had been taking two other 'first-novel' ladies to be presented to Shodbutt he had not taken her, though at the time she had not known who it was about whom her publisher was making such a fuss, as he hurried his 'authors' forward.

'Oh, so that is Mr Samuel Shodbutt?' is all she said.

'Yes. I've given him until eleven tonight to make me a reply about my book.'

'Have you? That's short notice. What fun.'

'It *may* be fun – for somebody! It may not. Time will tell.'

Nancy had been directing her little firefly eyes upon the occupants of the seats of honour in the high places, at the centre of things, surrounding the prime mover, Maisie Crook.

'Who is that funny boy talking to Mrs Crook – do you see who I mean?'

'*That?* That's Donald Butterboy.' Osorio Potter scowled and waved his hand in sovereign contempt. 'That's why we're all down here, didn't you know! He is to get the Book of the Week Prize for his book.'

'Indeed!' said little Nancy. 'I didn't know why we had been asked, but guessed it was something.' Nancy had thought all along it must be something to do with her and *Bursting Ripe*. 'My publisher told me to come and I came. I wouldn't have come if I had known it was for *that*!' she said, so disdainfully that Osorio looked at her in a little surprise.

CHAPTER 14

GOOD Night All! Never were words more ironically un-called for uttered, by any Midnight Uncle (or whatever the fellow is nicknamed who broadcasts the unctuous official farewell and tucks up the listener-in for the night), as it turned out; for this was to be such a night as few of the geniuses assembled beneath the roof of the hospitable Crooks are ever likely to forget — for it was to be, to put it mildly, a night of terror after all, in which Murder stalked abroad. Murder in his most hideous mood — as if almost Murder in person had wished to be of the party, so to speak, and to join in the fun — seeing there had been so much talk of him and his bloody doings, and of the money that his mere presence (in a book) assured the writer of even the most modest talents. Anyhow, whatever the motive, he stalked abroad. And the first that anyone knew of his visitation was a number of dull, but nevertheless distinct reports — *saccadés*, as Monsieur Jolat subsequently described them, next week at the Café du Dôme.

About two in the morning or a little later a bang-bang-banging occurred in the very centre of the Crook mansion, not so far from the apartment of Mrs Wellesley-Crook, in the region of the suites of honour, not far from the Royal Suite, occupied by Shodbutt. Then all was silence. But when you consider the number of ears gathered beneath this roof attuned, in theory if not in practice, to such an uproar — for whom this sinister *banging* meant all the difference between poverty and opulence, and who were past masters in extracting the last drop out of the sensational virtue in this un-mistakable sound, namely that of death-dealing small-arms, being inopinely discharged – and in extracting from bullet-riddled corpse after corpse, in a long series of 'mystery' stories, an ever fatter and fatter living – it is not surprising that these sounds did not go entirely unnoticed. In the rooms indeed in the immediate neighbourhood of that luxurious chamber from which they proceeded they resounded with an alarming loudness – which caused one of the most expert guests (as he hurried to the scene) to mutter grimly to his neighbour:

'There was no silencer on *that*.'

'You're right there, George!' the other said, with a dour professional chuckle.

To cut what would be a long story (in hands more stained with the ink of 'Crime' than mine) very short indeed, first one door opened, then another; and, after a little argument, it was decided by those scantily clothed bookworms who had gathered near the Crook apartment that a certain door was that of the room from which the ghastly sounds had come. It was the work of a moment to burst it open – indeed it was open already, all they had to do was to push it. And, switch-ing on the light as they entered, the half-dozen guests or so that had been the first on the spot stepped in and found Donald Butterboy dead in bed, with bullet wounds in several parts of his body, but mainly in the lumbar region. He was in bed – it was necessary to remove the clothes to ascertain all this and to locate the seat of the trouble. Two or three of the most eminent fictionists – and a critic covering nothing but murder yarns in his articles – were on all fours by this time, sniffing the carpet and peering under the four-poster. And it rapidly became a matter of common knowledge that from four holes in the mattress blood was streaming, down upon the carpet beneath the bed, where it was bringing into being four dark pools, for the cops to count when they arrived.

One guest took another aside in the death-chamber.

'What do you make of it, Gilbert?' he asked.

'If you ask me, Terence, he was shot *from underneath*.'

'How do you mean, Gilbert, *from underneath*?'

'Well, just what I say – from underneath – *the bed*.'

'My God!' exclaimed Terence, almost involuntarily.

'Mind you,' said Gilbert, 'it's only a guess. But it looks uncommonly like it.'

'How perfectly *fiendish*!' Terence whispered.

'Why?'

'Oh – I don't know! *From underneath!*'

'Well it looks like it, that's all I can say.'

'I'm afraid you're right, Gilbert, old man. I'm afraid you're right.'

The whole house-party, and the various categories of domestics, were at last roused, and the chamber-of-death became unpleasantly full. Voices had grown louder, as expert controversy increased in bitterness, and cigarette-smoke filled the air. The crowd parted, and Shodbutt, followed by Mrs S.S., the former in a sombrely magnificent best-selling dressing-gown, stalked to the bed. With wrinkled chin and furrowed forehead he stood and contemplated the defunct, the Butterboy that was. Another genius laid low! It was not the first he had seen, even of *dead* geniuses. How prodigal was nature – how careless of the single life! All this was megaphoned without words from his proudly dejected person. And as silently as he had come did he go, the crowd falling back as the none-too-popular Dictator of Letters marched to the door, shadowed out by the tiptoeing Joanie.

But a *second* banging, far louder than the first, now fell upon the ears of the overwrought Book-World. Bang-bang-

bang, and it went on in a menacing crescendo. 'The police!' exclaimed some. But the police had not had time to get out to Beverley Chase, at two in the morning. In very doubtful taste one of those present suggested 'The Murderer!' This was too much – one shattered Frothblower called out 'Shame!'

Such a salvo of bangs now broke out that all those in Butterboy's room rushed into the passage. The servants were engaged, it was discovered, in opening the much-be-chained manorial front-door. As it was dragged open two small figures in pale pink pyjamas entered the hall. They were two of the guests, who, under the impression that the house was on fire, and their minds full of many recent and often fatal incendiary fires in country seats, had jumped out of their first-floor window and landed in a flower-bed. Upon picking themselves up they had examined the house carefully, to detect tongues of flame, and were somewhat surprised not to see other guests hanging out of the windows or letting themselves down with sheets tied end to end. Then observing lights, and picking out shadows of apparently very collected figures upon blinds, they at length concluded that they had been mistaken, and that it was not a fire after all, but some other catastrophe – burglars, perhaps. They now felt it might be safer to be inside than out, so they knocked on the front door, with a violence that you would not have been led to expect of such a mild and undersized couple.

In the death chamber, which had filled up again, Sir Titus took Osorio by the arm and whispered: 'I do think it was very rough luck on Butterboy – just as he was going to be *crowned* too! I wonder who did it? Or was it suicide, do you suppose?'

'How could it be?'

'*It Takes Two to Make a Bedroom-Scene*, you think?'

'Such a scene as this, yes,' Osorio answered.

'Yes, I agree it would take some doing for a man to kill himself by shooting himself *from behind*.'

'Some burglar must have been beneath the bed.'

'Been surprised, I suppose, and hidden there: and then because poor Butterboy *would* not settle down, just plugged him through the mattress to send him to sleep, so that he might make his getaway.'

'That is possible. It must have been a burglar.'

'Not a professional, however, else he would have been more patient. What amazes me about burglars is their patience. My theory is it was one of the guests.'

Osorio shrugged his shoulders.

'They don't look capable of anything of that sort.'

'You're right there, they don't! I think, if we are to go by *appearances*, it lies between you and me!'

Osorio turned his head and smiled appreciatively at Sir Titus L'Estrange.

The crowd near the door was rudely hustled – the major-domo, fully dressed, was there, and he advanced towards the bed, followed by Mrs Wellesley-Crook, very tidy if not quite so fully dressed as her butler. Like Shodbutt she drew up at the foot of the bed and contemplated the corpse of her protégé from that position.

'You have telephoned the police and the physician?' she inquired of the major-domo, who said he had.

Then turning towards Osorio, who was standing with Sir Titus looking down at Butterboy, she said:

'Mr Potter, I want to speak to you! Will you come down with me, please?'

'Me?' asked Osorio.

'Yes, Mr Potter, please.'

'Ah ha!' whispered Sir Titus, squeezing Osorio's arm. 'You've been found out! Now for the Third Degree! Courage, Osorio!'

CHAPTER 15

'What a damned funny coincidence, Charlie, don't you think?'

'What is it?'

'That you of all people should have been called in on this case!'

With unaccustomed blandness, almost as disturbing as his standard misanthropy, Osorio beamed across the table at the 'Murderer' who saw him off at Paddington, and the 'Murderer' blinked back owlishly at him.

Mr Charles Dolphin, with more *cafard* than any disgruntled café-politician of the Third Republic, shrugged his large fat shoulders. In his professional capacity he put aside some of the graces of his private pessimism. He did not appear so much at his ease. He drew rank smoke in moody exhalations into the caverns of his lungs, and belched it forth again, out of his yellow-tipped nostrils.

His eyes were grave. They had lost their *sourire* – of the *pince-sans-rire* variety. They were dull and bloodshot. He was the picture of the man who is out of conceit with his job.

'Why shouldn't I be called in?' he asked a little truculently.

'It is a coincidence.'

'It is a coincidence. The detective has to accustom himself to coincidence. Until you become a detective you don't realize what a big part coincidence plays in human destiny.'

'Sometimes a *pleasant* part!' exclaimed Osorio, with a companionable smirk.

'Do you think so?' Charlie sighed. 'But there are not so many *reputable* private inquiry agents in London as you imagine. It was almost inevitable that I should be called in. Anyhow, here I am. And there are you.'

Osorio and his friend sat facing each other upon opposite sides of the luxuriously appointed writing-table – pencils dangling at the end of springed stalks of steel, red sponges in cut-glass baths to prevent cancer of the tongue – in the palatial library of Beverley Chase.

A typewritten list of the guests composing the house-party – which read like a little *Who's Who* of the Book-World – was on the table in front of Mr Dolphin. A steel-ringed reporter's note-book was open alongside the typed list. He had just written OSORIO POTTER at the top of a virgin page. He looked down at this name gloomily, and then he looked up at the young man with the ingratiating smirk lounging in the chair in front of him.

'So this, Ossie, was what you proposed I should undertake, was it?' he asked, yawning, the inexpressible boredom of the mastiff drooping in every line of his dewlap and corrugated brow.

'I don't understand you,' Ossie replied, with considerable dignity.

'What did I tell you to do, you fool? I advised you, didn't I, to throw that thing you showed me away? Why didn't you?'

He yawned again over the table at his friend, who was watching him with a gathering frown.

'Where is it now, by the way, Ossie?' he next asked, and looked down at the note-book. 'Got it on you, old lad? Or must we have a game of hide-and-seek?'

'What do you mean?' muttered Osorio. 'What are you talking about, Charlie?'

But Charlie proceeded without answering to write GAT

under OSORIO POTTER; and under that he wrote: 'Get him to hand it over or else he may shoot up the Crooks.' Then he looked up. He became stern.

'You know what I mean, sir. Where is your gun? In your pocket?'

All thoughts of making a good impression now flung to the winds, Osorio, flushing and scowling, was quite his old self again; and that was something gained, thought Charlie with a sigh.

'You're not accusing me of being *a murderer*, are you!' Osorio Potter exclaimed.

Charles Dolphin laughed in spite of himself at this.

'You don't make things very amusing for a detective, do you!' he said. 'A more boring case it would be difficult to imagine. There *is* no case in fact. When the message came through, I don't mind telling you, I felt inclined to telephone your hostess to have you taken into custody at once, as it was obviously you. It would have saved a lot of trouble. But of course I have to earn my keep – the Crooks are rich. But I wish you would bring this painful situation to an end.'

'But why me? Why pick on me? I was a great friend of Donald's.'

'Isn't it you? Mrs Crook says it was you.'

'Oh, *her*!'

'Everybody says it was you – and the whole Crime Club is here – they ought to know if anybody does. The police say it is. And you told me you were going to do it! What more do you want?'

'Don't be a fool – that was only a joke, Charlie. I was only ragging. You must see that.'

Charles Dolphin wrote mechanically.

'Stoutly denies charge. Give him the works.'

Then he looked up, and measured Ossie with a bilious eye.

'See here, old man, don't let's waste each other's time.'

'I agree!'

'I don't *like* sleuthing. I hate it. But you are coming between me and my bread-and-butter.'

'I see your difficulty, Charlie.'

Mr Dolphin smiled dismally.

'No, you flatter yourself – I didn't mean that. But everything points to you – why drag out the agony? Motive – opportunity: everything is there! Why not come clean, Ossie? It'll be better for you in the end and all that. Perhaps they'd send you to play ping-pong with Ronald True.'

'I'm much obliged. You're some *friend*, aren't you, Charlie!'

'But look – since I know who it is! What's the use of my getting all those people in and asking them a lot of damnfool questions. I know they're not murderers. They're not such fools as all that. You're the only simpleton in this outfit – and *you're the man*! And I'm here to get him! You can't get away from that!'

Osorio stood up, his hands clenched, and glaring at his fat and weary pal, who blinked in the glare but did not lower his eyes.

'You swine, Charlie! If I were not accused of murder I'd wring your bloody neck!'

'Consider it done! What then?'

'Why have I not been arrested? Because there's nothing against me! You haven't a scrap of evidence. You can't bluff me, Dolphin! I defy you! Do your worst!'

Charles Dolphin roused himself – he sat up, threatening energy in all his person.

'Very well. You insist on my turning this outfit upside-down, do you? Is that what I am to understand?'

'I don't care what you do, Mr Private Inquiry Agent.

That's what you're paid to do, I suppose. Why don't you do it?'

Charles flung himself back dramatically in his chair.

'Very well!' he thundered. 'You intend to make me pick about like an inquisitive chicken — to jack the tacks out of the armchairs and *rummage round* in the upholstery! You want to see me on all fours under Butterboy's bed, looking for your beastly fingerprints on the carpet! You want me to sniff in all the dirty tumblers to ferret out the sleeping-draught you probably did not administer — being too brutish to administer an anaesthetic to your prospective victim!'

'It's all one to me.' Osorio was now very cool and indifferent. 'But if you are *called in*, I suppose they will expect you to do a spot of work, and collect at least a *little* evidence. There's plenty of it lying about! You can't very well miss it.'

Charles Dolphin closed his mouth — he had been about to proceed with his declamation. He stared with great grimness but a shade of curiosity at Osorio, tapping his fountain-pen upon the table.

'Plenty of evidence?' he repeated. 'Where is it? I haven't seen any.'

'Look for it. I'm not the Sherlock. That's your job.'

Charles Dolphin continued in silence to bathe Osorio with a dreary gaze of long drawn-out and languid curiosity.

'Well,' he said at length. 'Sit down. Give me a line on it, I ask nothing better.'

Osorio Potter sat down, and took a packet of Weights out of his pocket.

'I don't want to hang you, Potter. Give me a list of suspects, if you have them.'

'I like that! You want me to do your stuff for you!'

'Aren't you prepared to do *something* on your side? You have a good deal at stake. I should have thought it would have been worth while.'

'Not at all. You have nothing against me. But what do you want?'

'Well, how about the Anglo-Indian baronet! Sir Titus —?'

'Oh, L'Estrange?' Osorio laughed scornfully. 'Of course, you would think of him first, Charlie, because you think he's so Secret Service!'

'Both bold and secret – Clubman exterior!'

'He didn't do it.'

'Why not? I've looked them over and he's my best bet – after you, Ossie.'

'You're a rotten detective.'

'That may be. But why must I let him out, your sinuous Sir Titus?'

'He's not *mine*.'

'I believe you are shielding him. He's really the perfect man for this sort of crime. He would in fact be better than yourself: if only we could pin it on to him.'

'You can't. He didn't do it!'

'How do you know?'

'Because I know who did.'

Charles Dolphin rose majestically to his full stature. He levelled his fountain-pen at Osorio's head.

'You know who did it?' he demanded, in a low and level voice.

'I do,' said Osorio unflinchingly.

'You are an accessory after the fact! Why did you keep back this information? Why did you not tell me at once?'

'I thought you could guess. I thought you knew.'

'Naturally I supposed it was you. Who was it then?'

'Mr Samuel Shodbutt of course.'

The mastiff features of the private detective relaxed, as if they had been ironed out, and they then gathered together again, to compose themselves ruggedly into an opposite expression. A heavy smile of sardonic appreciation bloomed sallowly where before all had been the winter of an inquiry-agent's discontent.

'Good egg!' Charles said.

Osorio beamed again upon his friend.

'Any evidence?' asked Charles.

'Of course. He's simply scattered clues about all over the place.'

'Capital! What sort?'

'Well, one of his gold cuff-links, for instance, is under the – er – fatal bed. I saw it.'

'Is it still there?'

'Probably, unless the chambermaid has pinched it. But I should search his room. It's no doubt teeming with clues.'

'Do you think so?'

'I'm sure of it, Charlie. You'd probably find the weapon.'

'What makes you think that!'

'I have a hunch.'

'Good. Send him in, will you?'

As Osorio was going towards the door, Charlie stopped him.

'Oh, a minute please. I had forgotten. *Motive!* What would you say was his motive?'

Osorio turned back, with a scowl of the most overwhelming scorn.

'Motive! Why isn't it plain enough? Are you blind, Charlie?'

'Well, what was it?'

'Shodbutt was going to give old Donald the Prize, wasn't he?'

'Well? I still do not see that that constitutes a motive.'

'At the last moment Shodbutt saw what a fool he would look: or Mrs Shodbutt explained to him. He couldn't face up to it! Donald had to disappear! *It Takes Two to Make a*

Bedroom-Scene!, as a Book of the Week Prize, would have been too much even for Shodbutt's reputation to survive.'

'*Oh!* Do you think so?'

'Have you seen the book?'

'No. I can't say I have.'

'You are not very thorough are you, Mr Dolphin! Have a look at it! – Well, Shodbutt panicked, that is evident. All Dictators are armed. Shodbutt was armed. The rest is simple.'

Charles Dolphin sat down at the table, turned over the page at which his note-book was open – the Osorio page – and wrote at the top of a fresh page: SAMUEL SHODBUTT.

'All right,' he said. 'I'll question him. Send him in.'

Three minutes later Samuel Shodbutt stalked stiffly into the Library.

'You asked to see me?' he inquired.

'Yes. Sit down, Mr Shodbutt. I have a few questions I should like to ask you. They are the usual routine questions. I shall not detain you long.'

Shodbutt sat down on the chair recently occupied by Osorio Potter and looked up, past his impending leaden lock, at the ceiling.

'You took a great interest in Donald Butterboy, Mr Shodbutt?'

'A *great* interest!' Shodbutt woke into a thunderous life immediately.

'You regarded him as a very gifted young man, Mr Shodbutt, did you not?'

But Shodbutt swelled as if Dolphin had asked him to breathe deeply and say *Ah*. There was a longish pause, what while he went on expanding. Then the answer came crashing forth.

'I regarded Butterboy, sir, as *a genius*!'

And having delivered himself of this fundamental shod-buttian utterance – words, certainly, which were no strangers to his lips, but to which his bust never apparently grew accustomed, since upon every fresh occasion it mobilized its bellows to do justice to them, and see to it these winged words did not lack wind – he sat quite still. He had expressed his faith in Genius. It was as if, with another man, he had just uttered his belief in God. And he eyed defiantly, challenging contradiction, this impertinent detective.

'You regard his book, Mr Shodbutt – this book, er, *It Takes Two to Make a Bedroom-Scene! ...*'

'That is its name, sir!'

'Yes. You regard this book as worthy of inclusion in your famous Book of the Week Club lists? As *absolutely* worthy of that honour?'

'Worthy of inclusion, sir!' trumpeted the outraged Shodbutt. He was for a moment speechless with outraged astonishment.

'*Worthy of inclusion*, sir!' he repeated incredulously. 'Why sir, there is no "Book Club" yet that would be worthy of *it*! I should have been compelled, sir, to have founded a new Club altogether – the Book of the Century Club – to have been able to offer such a masterpiece as Butterboy's a proper hospitality.'

Samuel Shodbutt flung back his head, and drew all the air in the room into his chest, until the walls seemed caving in, and coming up to stand close about him for his final exordium.

'*Book of the Week!*' he roared. 'It was merely absurd to call it a "book of the week"! It was such a book as only occurs once in a hundred generations!'

Charles Dolphin waited a moment, to see if any more remained to be said; then he made a note beneath the name of Shodbutt:

'He protesteth overmuch.'

Then he tapped the table sharply with his fountain-pen.

'Think again, Mr Shodbutt!' he said sternly.

'How do you mean, sir — *think again*!' the great man growled, regarding his cross-examiner with amazement.

'I am advised, Mr Shodbutt, that is all, that this book of Butterboy's was, in fact, a particularly foolish and even ridiculous production. I mean, sir, that it was of such an unspeakably inferior quality as would have made it in the highest degree compromising for you to include in it your weekly award stunt. I have reason to believe that it was a book of so patently stupid an order that even your weekly subscribers would have been certain to protest, and return it to you. And that your — reputation — would have suffered in consequence. Would you be prepared to endorse that view of the matter? Or do you still prefer to adhere to the fantastic opinions of this composition which you have just now expressed?'

Mr Samuel Shodbutt rose from the table, and Dolphin rose at the same time: he was quite prepared to catch him if he fell, for he was under the impression that the great Book-Dictator was about to have a stroke. But this was not the case.

'Sir!' Mr Shodbutt shouted. 'Your sources of information I can guess. I think I could name your "informants" without very much trouble!'

'Indeed! You prefer, I gather, to sustain your absurd contentions?'

'Sir, oblige me by confining yourself to what your functions prescribe. But I would not in any case be expected to sit here and listen to these insults directed against the dead! It is outrageous! If *you* have no respect for dead genius — for genius foully done to death — and in your profession one does not look for *respect* of any sort! — I *have*, sir. I shall listen to you no longer! You are not only a detective but a cad!'

As he took a step to remove himself from this scurrilous sleuth, Charles Dolphin placed his hand upon Shodbutt's arm.

'Mr Shodbutt. Before you go, please. Have you lost a gold cuff-link by any chance?'

Shodbutt glared at him.

'Yes, I have!'

'Ah, I thought so.'

'Perhaps you will be good enough to tell me where I can find it.'

'Certainly. You were so careless, Mr Shodbutt, as to leave it under Donald Butterboy's bed.'

Shodbutt's eyes slowly took on an expression of terrified blankness, as he realized the full implication of the discovery of his property under Butterboy's bed.

'What n-n-nonsense is this?' he stuttered.

'It is not nonsense. Tell me, Mr Shodbutt, are you armed?'

'Armed! What for?'

'Oh, nothing, Mr Shodbutt. I must ask you to wait here for a short while. I shall have to go up to your apartments and make a search.'

'But this is an outrage!' Shodbutt stood stuttering beneath the unsympathetic eye of the melancholy Dolphin. 'A search! This is unheard of! I shall at once telephone to the Chief Constable of Oxfordshire!'

But Charles Dolphin moved closer to him and, pointing to the chair at the table and fixing him with an eye of policemanesque menace, almost hissed:

'Cut that out, Shodbutt! Go back to that chair!'

As if apprehending some violence, or conceiving the proximity of handcuffs, Shodbutt, a little short of breath, resumed his seat, remarking in a high-pitched snarl as he sat down:

'Very well, young man! You are obeyed! I call you to witness that I submit to your instructions, and I shall observe them to the letter.'

'In that you are wise, and are somewhat effacing the bad impression made upon me by your recent violence.'

A pathetic phantom of a dictatorial snort echoed behind Charlie as he rapidly left the library.

Five or six minutes later, upon his return, Mr Shodbutt was in the same position in which he had left him. His mouth was, however, hanging a little loosely open, the long runaway chin of the Book-Dictator was more wrinkled and his eyes had a somewhat far-away look. His mind was absenting itself from the troublous present whether into the glorious past or the vengeful future it was impossible to say.

Charles Dolphin sat down in front of him, and placed dramatically two objects upon the table: an outsize automatic pistol, and a gold cuff-link.

'Exhibit A,' he announced sombrely, 'a gold cuff-link. Your property, sir: am I right?'

Shodbutt nodded.

'Exhibit B. One automatic pistol. Likewise your property, Mr Shodbutt?'

Shodbutt shook his head.

'*Not* your property? But I have just taken it, sir, from the top drawer of the tallboy in your bedroom.'

The deflated and dreamy Dictator gave a curious, almost mischievous grin. He croaked thinly, cocking a quizzical eye at his accuser: 'S-s-somebody must have put it there. It is not mine.'

'That remains to be seen.'

'Not at all!' stammered Shodbutt. 'Even if it were mine it makes no difference.'

'How is that, Mr Shodbutt?'

'I have an alibi,' Mr Samuel Shodbutt almost whispered over the table.

Dolphin seemed a little taken aback at this. Alibi! He did not appear to have allowed for the possibility of Shodbutt's movements at the relevant time being satisfactorily accounted for. But he quickly recovered.

'Your wife, I suppose!' he snapped.

'No,' muttered Shodbutt. 'No!'

'Not your wife?'

'No,' answered Shodbutt faintly.

'May I have the name of the person whose statement will constitute the alibi, according to you?'

Shodbutt, who remained in the same at once shrivelled and detached attitude, his hands folded on his lap, shot him a queer, faint ironical glance out of the corners of his eyes.

'She will be here in a minute,' he said. 'I have sent her a message, asking her to come.'

At that moment the door burst open, and Baby Bucktrout entered the library.

'Ah, Miss Bucktrout!' sighed Samuel Shodbutt demurely. 'Please inform this gentleman, who accuses me of killing Donald Butterboy, that I couldn't have done it, will you. Seeing that I was in your company at the time.'

Baby Bucktrout advanced, with great decision, towards the table.

'Of course he was – all the evening!' she called out as she came forward. 'What on earth are you talking about! You must be off your rocker to accuse Mr Shodbutt – of a crime – of *that* sort. He's as gentle as a lamb! It's perfectly disgusting!'

Casting a grateful, tender and contented glance in the direction of Baby Bucktrout, Samuel Shodbutt still sat with his hands folded in his lap. Dolphin sat staring heavily from one to the other. His glance was particularly piercing as it fed upon the person of the insolent débutante. He did not disguise what a low opinion he had of Shodbutt's alibi. But for the moment silence reigned.

Such was the tableau that met the irritable and imperious eye of Mrs Wellesley-Crook (of the Crooks of Chicago, and on her mother's side a Toyt – the solid Virginian Toyts, not the nomadic Toyts that can be found anywhere from Seattle to Santa Fé) as under full sail she entered the apartment a moment later.

'What nonsense is this, Mr Dolphin?' she exclaimed, coming up to him haughtily. 'Will you be so good as to explain yourself?'

Charles Dolphin rose with all the majesty of the Law, and confronted this upstart Crook and Toyt, his long fingers supporting him fanwise upon the table.

'I owe you no explanation, Mrs Wellesley-Crook. It is my business to get to the bottom of this sinister mystery. And in the course of my investigations I have encountered up to the present, a great deal of opposition. This man,' indicating Shodbutt, 'has, to say the least, been exceedingly obstructive.'

'Mr Dolphin! Will you kindly return to London at once! We shall require your services no longer. I learn from my butler – who took the precaution of informing himself, by means of observations directed from a position at the key-hole – that Mr Potter is a friend of yours. You have been sitting and gossiping here with the murderer of poor Butter-boy, instead of gathering the necessary evidence to effect his arrest.'

'Your major-domo, madam got but a bird's-eye view of the scene, from the keyhole, and has conveyed to you a distorted picture of what occurred.'

'I shall not pay your firm. And I shall report you to the police!'

'I, madam, I shall report you, for sheltering a homicidal maniac, and attempting to defeat the ends of justice!'

Mrs Wellesley-Crook turned her back upon Charles Dolphin, and she was as impressive behind as she was in front, if not more so.

'Come, Mr Shodbutt,' she commanded. 'I must apologize to you for the conduct of this *person*. Come, Baby, my peach! This matter will be left in the hands of the police. If they refuse to arrest Potter that is their own business. I shall do no more about it. But he shall not remain under this roof any longer!'

Mrs Wellesley-Crook was not seen again by any of her guests, and at eight o'clock next morning the servants intimated to all the company individually that buses and cars would be ready at the door to take them to the station at 10.50 and would they be so good as to pack at once? Their visit was at an end. And at 10.30, like a Witches' Sabbath, the Book-World were swept out into the crowded conveyances provided for them, and vanished in clouds of dust from the neighbourhood of Beverley Chase – all except Shodbutt, who, with feelings which not only beggared description but defied words, walked down with Mrs S.S. to the station, and tipped the station master with a five-pound-note to secure him a first-class carriage immediately the train entered the station, and to lock him in; which that personage did according to plan, in the twinkling of an eye, and the Book-World clamoured in vain to get into his carriage, for the train was full to capacity.

Seated facing the engine, in his first-class compartment, Samuel Shodbutt committed himself to no statement, however trivial, for a long time; and Mrs S.S. looked out of the window, and words did not come easily to her either, for her indignation at the treatment of her lord and master was, if not as deep as his, yet more primitive and beyond the reach of words. But at last S.S., without picking his phrases, decided that the moment had come to pass a remark. And he passed it with a rather threatening look, as if she had asked for it and he was passing it, in accordance with her wish – a very heavy remark indeed.

'Well, if *that* doesn't teach us to make ourselves cheap, all I can say is that *nothing* will!'

'Nothing!' said Mrs S.S. 'I could murder that woman.'

'Enough murder has been done for one day. But I shall write her such a ripsnorter when I get back as she won't forget in a hurry, I can tell you, the ill-bred old Yank!'

'Ill-bred! I could wring her neck.'

'Anyhow, she's lost her Butterboy.'

'She'll soon find another.'

'Yes, but just let her come to me about *him*! I'll tell her to stick him up . . .'

'Yes, you certainly *will* – I'll see to that!'